CW00377175

Puzzle

at

Peacock Perch

A Secret Senior Sleuths Society Mystery

by Suzanne Rudd Hamilton

large print edition

Based on the play *Puzzle at Peacock Perch*
by Suzanne Rudd Hamilton

Suzanne Rudd Hamilton

Puzzle at Peacock Perch: Copyright © 2021 by Suzanne Rudd Hamilton

ISBN: 9798764147833

Imprint: HHH Press

Meet the Secret Senior Sleuths Society

Why have one detective when you can have a whole secret society? This group of seniors is making time amid their bridge and mahjong tournaments, bingo games, arts and crafts, and tennis and pickle ball matches to solve mysteries together in their community.

Each chapter features a different detective and their team trying to decipher and investigate the clues they've found. They put all the knowledge from their former occupations to work together to crack the case. Their code names are:

 Madame Sleuth

Presiding investigator, founder of the society and head busybody. She's from New England.

 Daring Detective

A Midwestern mother, housewife and mystery book aficionado.

Captain Cluemaster

Career Army officer and former military police.

 Inspector Instinct

Former forensic government accountant from Washington D.C.

 Newshound

Past newspaper reporter and editor from California.

 Magnolia Mastermind

Former beauty queen and debutant from Georgia.

 Chemical Cluist

Former chemist who worked in Michigan for a major tire manufacturer.

 Delta Snoops

Owned a small general store in rural Alabama.

 Private Eyes

From southern California, a new member of the group, who hasn't revealed her former occupation.

Queens Quister

A lifetime New Yorker from Queens who taught inner-city kids.

 Master Mayhem

A building contractor from Illinois and the self-elected comedian of the group.

 Sherley Sparks

Former electrician from rural Missouri.

 Mystery Minx

A part-time children's librarian from Kansas.

 Sir Red Herring

Rich. Old money from Massachusetts. Never really worked.

 Smoking Gun

Nobody knows where he's from or what he did for a living.

Behind the Pages

Full disclosure, I live in a senior active adult community in sunny Florida. It's great.

After living my whole life in the Chicago area, I was charmed at the collection of people from all over the world. There were Southerners, Midwesterners, New Englanders, New Yorkers, Canadians, Australians and Europeans, all living together. The varying cultures and differences were a refreshing change.

The other revelation was the vast experiences and knowledge from their former occupations. It was like a giant think tank. If you needed to know something, no matter what it was—from rocket science to exotic plants—chances are someone had done that for a living.

And with all the community activities, everyone spent a lot of time together. It soon became clear to me that there were very few secrets.

So, during the pandemic, I wrote an interactive whodunit play, with the help of our small community theater group, which lampooned how the gossip mill, both verbal and on social media, can take on a life of its own and help solve a mystery. Since we performed it on Zoom, attendees played detective in small groups and discussed clues and suspects. That gave birth to the *Secret Senior Sleuths Society.*

And in this book series, I can delve into the process of the detective work more with its twists and turns and explore the suspects, learn more about what motivates the detectives and take a peek at what it's like to live in a typical American senior community. It's probably not what most people expect of a retirement community.

It's an interesting examination of a micro-society, although somewhat exaggerated, and how word-of-mouth can skew perspectives.

Suzanne Rudd Hamilton

Chapter 1

The Case:

Madame Sleuth

Senior communities were not what they seemed to be. On the outside, people thought it was a slow-paced life with bingo, bridge and billiards all the time, but it was a facade. I've lived in Peacock Perch for ten years and I could attest to the antics and amateur intrigues here every day.

For years, I kept my ears open and my eyes on everyone and everything. I have stacks of notebook logs uncovering betrayal, bombastic deceptions, blasphemous libel, many breaches of the peace, illegal betting, bribery, and some petty burglary, to name a few. So I searched the community for the best and the brightest to create the Secret Senior Sleuths Society, a clandestine collection of clue finders and case busters, under my close direction and supervision, to crack open the illicit capers here in "the perch."

Our society was secret, as we must stealthily move within and investigate. I hand-selected several superior individuals who have shown an aptitude for puzzles and possess particular skills and exceptional experience to produce results. We all have code names to conceal our real identities to the rest of the people in "the perch."

And now, we have a genuine case to solve, a real puzzler. This was a true testament to my genius and leadership.

Scuttlebutt revealed one of our residents, Willow Wisteria, was missing. It was up to us to track down the truth of what happened to her and why.

The team has arrived. I will make my grand entrance and announce our task.

"Welcome to the Secret Senior Sleuths Society. I am Madame Sleuth, the presiding investigator. I am pleased to announce we have a novice newcomer in our midst, so I will explain our primary principle to you and as a reminder to us all—Secrecy, Sleuthing and Success."

"Our next order of business is a new case. It's a prophetic puzzler. I've named it "The Case of the Vanishing Vixen." I have a flair for alliteration, don't you think?"

"Our vixen in this case is Willow Wisteria. Since we constantly monitor the Mugbook and Nosy Neighbors social media apps for intelligence information, we have noticed a high number of posts discussing Willow's disappearance."

"Did anyone drag the ponds?" Master Mayhem joked.

"Ahem. Master Mayhem. That form of jocularity is neither helpful nor honored. This is a detective society; perhaps you should start a "jesters" club if you wish to be a comedian. I am sure they will appreciate your prurient peculiarities more than we do," I ordered.

"Now, as I was saying, the missing person is one of the single women members of Peacock Perch who lives in the Parrot condominiums. Based on reports, she is not well-liked in the community. Preliminary investigation reveals that she is disagreeable, distasteful and even detested by some people."

"That could make the investigation both easy and difficult at the same time. It means she may have a lot of enemies to suspect, but not a lot of friends to provide information," Captain Cluemaster said.

"That could work in our favor," Daring Detective offered. "While family and friends can often be the primary source for details regarding whereabouts, habits and personal information, but since she's alienated most of the people in 'the perch,' absolutely everyone is talking about her."

"Seems like we're jumping the gun. Maybe she's on vacation or visiting someone. People come and go a lot around here. Has anyone checked her condominium? How do we even know she's missing?" Sir Red Herring asked.

"Sir Red Herring, if we knew all the answers, there would be no need to investigate!" I responded.

"Now, if I may continue. Since our victim was prolifically involved in groups and activities in the area, there should be plenty of paths to follow to decipher and deduce clues. And thanks to our handy retired electrician, Sherly Sparks, secret cameras have been placed all over Peacock Perch and we have hours of gossip footage to review."

"Madame, what's all this about cameras? Isn't that an invasion of privacy?" Inspector Instinct objected.

"I'm not comfortable with cameras, Madame; we never discussed that. They need to be taken down immediately, and the footage needs to be destroyed," Daring Detective objected.

"It was my executive decision as presiding investigator. Just the social media posts were not enough, so we needed a little reconnaissance. Besides, they are hidden cameras, so no one will ever know they are being filmed," I explained.

"Madame, we all represent this society, not you alone. I believe we should take a vote to destroy the cameras. All in favor?" Sir Red Herring asked and everyone raised their hands.

"Good heavens, people, this is a sleuths society, not a knitting circle. This is an investigation; we are going to have to break a few eggs and a few rules to get to the truth," I rebutted and saw most of the groups' hands raised.

"Madame, I believe you've been outvoted," Herring said. "Please have the cameras removed."

"It's not as though we are broadcasting the secret footage on the 'interweb' or anything. You can hear any of this gossip just sitting at the pool for a day. But very well, I believe they could have been a great asset to us, but I will have them removed," I reluctantly conceded.

"Now then, I divided you into teams to review the camera footage from each location. You need to isolate the potential clues and prospective suspects and use the social media posts we've collected to identify the motive, means and opportunity for the misdeed," I said.

"Or not. There may be no crime here. How long has this person been missing?" Smoking Gun asked.

"According to my sources, we can isolate the time of the disappearance to between two and four weeks ago. No one notified the police as yet because there is no certainty of a crime. But eventually someone will report her missing, so we don't have a lot of time to acquire leads," I explained.

"Two to four weeks? That's a huge gap. The trail is cold," said Smoking Gun.

"Now, that's not the appropriate attitude! We must solve this case. The timing is a question, part of the mystery we must resolve. The accounts from the people and the posts vary greatly, but the truth will come out in our investigation," I responded.

"I think this sounds like a lot of fun," Master Mayhem said.

"I assigned each of you a team. Magnolia Mastermind will work with Sherly Sparks, Newshound and Delta Snoops. Captain Cluemaster, you can work with Mystery Minx and Master Mayhem—good luck, you'll need it. Inspector Instinct, you and Sir Red Herring are with Queens Quister. And Daring Detective can bring our new member into the fold with Chemical Cluist. And Smoking Gun, you will…"

"I work alone," Smoking Gun said abruptly and lit a cigar.

"Exactly. I divided the accounts by area, distributed to each team and will disseminate the dossiers. Of course, to protect the innocent and the guilty, all the names in the dossiers and camera footage have been altered with pseudonyms. Since spring has sprung, I took the lead from our victim's name and I thought flower names would be delightful to hide the identities of the suspicious," I reported.

"Daring Detective, you will investigate the reports at the community pool and the Slippery Sandals bar. There are some interesting accusations on both the film and in media posts that require interviews and further inspection.

Captain Cluemaster, I believe your military tactics will serve us well at the victim's residence. There are several issues there that are particularly peculiar. I need a covert operation there to identify the true and false information.

Magnolia Mastermind, I have a simple task for you. You spend so much time in the card and arts rooms, you know everyone. Follow up on the fanciful accusations and put your master blabbermouth to work and see if you can dig up any more dirt."

"Well, bless your heart, Madame." Magnolia shot a sideways glance and winked.

"Inspector Instinct, we need your accounting expertise to follow the money to see if it leads us anywhere. This will require a deep dive.

And finally, Smoking Gun, I also need you to follow up on some posts about a mysterious accident, which may or may not be related. There are some puzzling reports that make little sense. I need your particular set of skills to uncover any relationships, so to speak.

Report any findings back to me immediately. As presiding investigator, I will coordinate all the data and advise each of you of any avenues that require additional analysis. There are many intersecting and overlapping layers to this mystery and plenty of rumors to examine and eliminate," I instructed.

"Thank goodness for the never-ending stream of nonsensical chatter in our community to give us plenty of rumors and reports to query. Remember to tread carefully when interviewing the suspects—I mean people—we didn't want to tip them off.

Everyone is dismissed. Remember, everything is hearsay until it is proven. No one in this community is above suspicion and no one can be trusted—except our group, of course. Happy hunting!" I said.

Chapter 2

The Pool:

Daring Detective

I was excited about an actual case to investigate. I always thought of myself as a homespun detective. After all, I spent my life as a mother and housewife, so I had no real training. But when I read detective novels or saw whodunnits, I always knew the culprit right away. I guess it's a sixth sense.

I grew up reading Nancy Drew and Hardy Boys books. I always dreamed of being a detective. I used to go around my neighborhood trying to solve every little puzzle. The case of the missing bike and the dilemma of the disappearing Halloween candy were just kids causing trouble, but I solved the case and caught each perpetrator.

And when my kids misbehaved, I became a master at interrogation. I always got them to crack. I had a way of talking to people and getting them to spill the beans.

When we moved here, I was glad to find some fellow mystery book buffs. Madame led the group and would never let us read the end of the book, so we could have rousing discussions about who we thought did it. Then she told us how it ended.

That was a bit frustrating, and some read the end ahead of the meetings and pretended they didn't, but I'm a mystery addict; I wanted to figure out the end myself.

It was obvious we had some deep thinkers in the group with a wide range of knowledge. We went to mystery plays and shows to try out our skills firsthand. That was fun. Everyone here fancied themselves a master detective.

Then Madame caught wind of the theft of some toilet paper and coffee supplies in our recreational center, so she decided there was trouble afoot. Next thing I knew, we were a secret sleuths society tasked with solving the crime. It wasn't that hard, but it was a start. There were a lot of rumors swirling around, so we figured out the potential suspects and followed them until we caught them red-handed. "The Case of the Sticky-Fingered Senior" was solved.

Madame smelled a mystery everywhere. I heard she actually tailed people here in the perch just to find out if they were up to anything nefarious. She created drama. She doesn't have a lot to do. But I like the group. It was fun and interesting how everyone's knowledge and experiences came together to solve puzzles.

Now it looked like a real case fell into our lap. This was going to be a lot of fun.

"Ok team. We need to sift through the wreckage of these social media posts and the secret camera footage, so get comfortable. Take a look at the posts in the dossier and we'll get the video started," I said. "Master Mayhem has kindly agreed to help us with the computer to review the video camera footage."

"Daring Detective, is it? I'm new to this game. My name is Do… Oops, I mean, my detective name is Senora Sleuth… or Private Eyes. What do you think?" she said.

"You'd better go with Private Eyes. Madame will have a conniption if anyone's name is even close to hers. The names are a little silly, but it lends to the mystique and makes everyone feel like a detective in a 'secret' society. Madame likes the names, so we all just went along. At least we talked her out of the daily code words, for now," I explained.

"I will have it cued up in a minute," Master Mayhem said.

"We're looking at two incidents Madame wants us to investigate," I said. "The first one is at the pool and the second one is at the pool bar. In the dossiers folders, there's a transcript of each recording. Madame had someone transcribe them for future reference. To protect the identity of the gossipers, each person in every video has been labeled simply A through D to denote the different people. If you know or recognize any of these people, please keep it to yourself. If we're going to sort this out, we need to keep it professional. Please take notes on anything that seems worth following up on."

"Do you ever feel bad snooping on your neighbors like this?" Private Eyes said.

"I did at first, but the information we gather is no different from spending a few hours listening to the chatter at the bar or reading the social media forums. Gossip in this community bounces off the walls like in a bubble and nothing stays a secret for long. Plus, if we can help someone by solving a mystery, the ends justify the means," I explained.

"Ok, I'm ready to roll," Mayhem said and started the recordings.

"Madame has labeled this first recording as *Slippery Sandals Slope* which features two women talking at the pool bar. I know the names are silly, but Madame loves her alliterations. I think it makes her feel like an old-time detective," I laughed.

"She is an old-time detective," Mayhem joked.

"Ok, let's see what we can do with all this," I said.

A: That was a good game.

B: Yeah. And it was so peaceful without Willow arguing every call. I wish she wasn't in our league. She's too competitive.

A: Oh, you didn't hear? No one's seen Willow in weeks.

B: Really? I hate to say this, but maybe she finally ticked off the wrong person.

A: So she argues a lot. Are you suggesting that someone would harm her for that? No way. And besides, no one even knows what happened to her.

B: Well, if someone did kill her, I wouldn't be surprised if it was Buck, the bartender.

A: Ok, you're cut off—you're talking crazy.

B: No, really. She's very mean to the servers here and one of them told me she never tips. I've seen her loudly berate them if her drink is not just right.

A: They're so nice here and anyway, no one would...

B: Oh no? My neighbor said she pitched a hissy fit right in front of everyone just a couple of weeks ago because they wouldn't serve her. She was drunk and called Buck an incompetent idiot who couldn't pour a drink right, even if it came from a can. And she said she was going to get him fired.

A: But come on, how...

B: It wouldn't take much to poison those Moscow mules she's always drinking.

A: Well, I guess, but still, no one would do that.

B: You never know. She's missing, isn't she?

"This next recording is called *The Sad Stalker* with two gentlemen talking at the pool, " I said.

A: Oh, there's that (Binny Buttercup) trying to impress the women again with his tan and his Speedo. He's quite the playboy around here, you know.

B: Really? I hadn't heard that. I see him around a lot. He seems like a sweet guy. But I do wish he'd wear longer swim trunks; some things you just can't unsee.

A: Oh yeah, wherever the single ladies are, you'll find him dancing or playing cards, golf, tennis, Bocce ball. He seems to be everywhere.

B: That's nice; he's popular.

A: You could say that, but it goes too far.

B: What do you mean?

A: Well, I've seen him cozy up to a couple of different single women around here, but the worst is him and Willow Wisteria. He follows her around like a puppy dog, buying her drinks and opening doors for her.

B: Oh, I know Willow. I've played pickleball with her. Now that you mention it, I have seen them together here at the pool a few times. He was putting sunscreen on her or something. Are they dating?

A: Depends on who you ask. If you ask Willow, she says no. But if you ask (Binny), he says yes. She's not even nice to him, but he won't go away. At the dance last month, he was in a huff because she brought a young man and they were all over each other on the dance floor. He was so jealous; he told my friend's husband that he could never forgive her betrayal and she'd be sorry.

B: Wow, really?

"Ok, there's some information we can sink our teeth into. Let's talk suspects. Remember, any suspect needs to have motive, means and opportunity," I explained.

"Isn't it obvious? Binny Buttercup did it," Private Eyes said. "Willow rejected him and he threatened her. You know what they say, hell hath no fury like a man scorned."

"I thought that only the women scorned were furious," Mayhem joked.

"It works both ways," I corrected. "(Buttercup) could be a suspect on the basis of motive, but we have no idea of his means or opportunity."

"Maybe he did her in with poison sunscreen?" Mayhem laughed.

"Poison is a real possibility. I'm a retired chemist and I can create any number of toxins out of easily attainable ingredients that can kill someone slowly or quickly, depending on the dosage. Poison is a preferred method of murder as it is easy, convenient and can often be masked or attributed to other ailments," offered Chemical Cluist.

"I knew it, it's that Buck the bartender. He poisoned her Moscow mule. Willow's right—he can't pour a drink," Mayhem laughed.

"I like the drinks at the bar," countered Cluist.

"Aww, you wouldn't know a mojito from a margarita," Mayhem argued.

"Ok, everybody, let's not get distracted. Private Eyes, is there anything in the social media sweep that lends any information?" I asked.

"Well, yes," she said, clicking the computer keys. "There's a lot of chatter on the Mugbook page and Nosy Neighbors about Willow's argument with the bartender. The names were all deleted, but I do have the text of the posts…

Did anyone see Willow at the bar? She was falling-down drunk and abusive to the bartender. She should be banned from the bar.

I hate to say this, but I was there and I think I saw someone put something in her drink. I don't know, though, she was screaming and ranting about something.

No one here would do that! If someone is drunk and abusive, they definitely should not be allowed in the bar.

That's a lousy way to get customers. They definitely won't come back if they're dead. Lol.

"Well, there's your smoking gun right there," Mayhem said.

"That's just gossip. We don't know if this person had a grudge against Willow. You can't fully trust what you read in these posts," Chemical Cluist argued.

"Look, I'm new to the community and this group, but I would think we need to take all evidence into consideration," Private Eyes interjected sheepishly.

"I agree with all of you; social media may be the bane of existence, but people talk about things they wouldn't say face to face, so we need to give it some weight," I said.

"I'll dig into the poison possibilities and look for a poison that can either be applied topically or ingested. There are a lot of variables with poison... application requirements, time limits, host substances, and lethal percentages of success are all factors to consider," Cluist said.

"Good. Private Eyes and I will interview some of these people to see if we can get any clues. This is not a lot to work on. Let's see what we can unearth," I said, and the boys left.

Daring Detective

I couldn't wait to dig into this case. The bartender could be a suspect; he had means and opportunity. And if Willow was mean to the staff and didn't tip, anyone at the bar could have the same motive, means and opportunity. It's easy to add poison into a drink.

The biggest problem was the lack of a body. We didn't even know if we have a murder on our hands. Willow was just missing. But in missing person cases, Police often believed that if the victim isn't recovered in a few days, then it's likely foul play—and she's been gone for at least a couple of weeks. So, at this point, we needed to treat this as a murder so we could propose or eliminate potential suspects.

I still couldn't believe that anyone here in our little slice of paradise could be a possible killer, but there is no utopian existence. Sometimes even good people could be pushed to the edge.

Without a body or a weapon, we had to build the case based on anecdotal evidence and, as much as it pained me, social media was a big part of that. Our team assignment offered a few suspects—Binny Buttercup and the bartender or staff of Slippery Sandals. They all had motive and maybe means and opportunity, but everything we had was circumstantial.

I didn't know much about Binny Buttercup. I went to the pool sometimes and frequented the weekly outdoor DJ parties, so I might have seen him. There are a few men who dance with all the ladies. They're harmless, but I didn't pay much attention to them. Now I needed to know everything about all of them.

Our first stop was the pool area. Especially in Florida's year-round good weather, the pool was the hub of the community. It was a decent-sized scalloped pool in the center of a sea of lounge chairs and tables and was surrounded by a lazy river where people glided along on tubes and escaped the heat. Few people swam; mostly people just stood in the pool and chatted. Some played cards at tables around the pool and some lounged and tanned. But everyone in the community came through the pool area, eventually.

The outdoor pool bar, Slippery Sandals, adjacent to the pool, had a surfing beach theme with big surfboards on either side of the huge bar that listed the food and drinks offered. Over the bar was a thatched roof, like a tiki hut, and the front of the bar had a mural of cresting waves. Even all the chair backs looked like towels.

Many sat at the bar or surrounding tables and ate, talked, or watched sporting events on TV, but the main attraction for ladies at the bar was Buck the bartender.

He was a young, tall, tan, good-looking man with long sweeping golden hair and an award-winning smile. That helped when you worked for tips.

There were always a lot of ladies gaggling around the bar, smiling and joking with him or just gazing at him from their nearby pool chairs. People called them the "sunscreen groupies." I could hardly blame them; he was very good looking. And contrary to Master Mayhem's opinions, most people thought he made the best mixed drinks around.

"How are we going to interview the suspects without them knowing we're working on a case?" Private Eyes asked.

"We'll just talk to them and covertly bring up Willow," I said. "Trust me, I have six children and ten grandchildren. I know how to find out who's guilty. Let's start with the bartender. Follow my lead."

At the bar, we found Buck behind the bar with his adoring groupies filling most of the stools, but found a couple of open seats.

"Hi, Buck, I don't know what drink to order. Can you make some recommendations?" I asked to loosen him up to talk.

"The drink list is on the wall. It's a hot day, so a lot of people like the frozen drinks, but I can make anything you want," Buck said.

"You mentioned before that you wanted that drink your friend told you about. It was called a donkey or something?" Private Eyes winked and smiled to Daring.

"Yes, that was Willow Wisteria. Do you remember her, Buck? She always had the same drink. I can't remember what it was called."

When I innocently asked about Willow's drink, Buck's smile turned into a frown.

"Yes, I remember. Moscow mules," he said and looked down.

"That's right." I smiled at him, but both Private Eyes and I watched him closely while he made the drinks. He never made eye contact with us after that and didn't smile when he handed us our drinks.

"Excuse me, but I overheard you talking to the bartender about... well... Willow," a lady abruptly whispered to us without warning. We didn't even see her approach.

It was one of the sunscreen groupies. She was well-tanned wearing big sunglasses and a floppy hat. They were never far away from Buck and were often eavesdropping.

This was a stroke of luck. Now we could see how Buck reacted to gossip about Willow. Guilty people often avoided eye contact and conversations when they wanted to evade something. My kids always stayed away from me whenever they did something wrong.

"Yes, I just remembered Willow always talked about these Moscow mules."

When I responded to the lady, I couldn't help but notice Buck moved right by us and cleaned up the well area in front of the bar with his head down. He was listening.

"I thought if you were her friend, you may have some news about her. Everyone's wondering what happened to her," the lady said.

"I wouldn't say friends. We just played cards twice, and she talked about these delicious Moscow mules that Buck made. Did you know her?" Private Eyes interjected.

"I've seen her around, especially here at the pool bar—if you know what I mean," the lady said and looked at Buck with disapproval.

The lady left and Buck quickly walked to the other side of the bar.

"Did you see the bartender move away from us?" Private Eyes said suspiciously.

"Yes, I did. Very astute. He definitely wanted to hear what she had to say. I think he's hiding something," I said.

I poured my drink into the plant next to the bar and waved Buck down for a refill. I needed to get him to open up about Willow. Maybe he'd trip up and spill something other than drinks if we kept mentioning her.

"Willow was right; you make a wonderful Moscow mule. She talked about it all the time. She must have been one of your best customers."

Buck handed me the drink, grimaced and shuddered a little at the mention of her name, like he was disgusted. But then he hurried to the other side of the bar.

Suddenly, Private Eyes knocked over her drink and Buck came running over with a bar rag.

"Sorry, I'm so clumsy," she said and winked at me.

"Look, Buck, I know you aren't supposed to tell tales about owners, but don't worry, Willow is no friend of mine. I heard she was mean to the staff and didn't tip. I hate people who abuse our staff," I prodded.

"Me, too. You guys work so hard; no one should be unkind," Private Eyes added.

Buck shook his head. "I don't want to talk about other residents, but she tried to get me fired because I wouldn't… you know."

"She hit on you?" Private Eyes and I leaned in, hanging on his every word.

"Yes. It's really awkward now that everyone says she's missing. People keep looking at me strangely and I even heard someone say I poisoned her drink. But that's not true. She kept grabbing my hand and tried to kiss me. She even leaned over the bar once and pinched my butt when I was serving another customer. When I asked her to stop, she said she was going to tell the manager I was inappropriate to her," he confessed.

"Wow, how horrible," Private Eyes said.

So Buck had a secret, but it wasn't what anyone thought. The ladies gossiping in the footage just made assumptions based on what they heard and thought they saw.

"Well, I guess he's off the list," Private Eyes said.

"Yep, just typical gossip trails that lead to nothing. Look, I think that's Mr. Buttercup. Let's go over to the pool and see what we can find out about him."

Those men talking about Binny Buttercup in the video footage were sure right. There he was at the corner of the pool doing pull-ups on the pool ladder, trying to impress some female onlookers. Watching him pull himself up and down on the ladder handles, while smiling and waving to the ladies was a little lame and sad, to be honest. Some of them waved back at him, but I didn't think his attempt at muscular prowess could impress any of them. But it was an innocent game.

Binny was a decent-looking trim older man with a nice tan, but he wore a bikini Speedo. All the other men were in long shorts swimsuits. Even if he was a perfect Adonis specimen, which he wasn't, it just made me feel uncomfortable. I didn't know why. It shouldn't, but I had a tendency to look away.

We sat in pool chaises next to two of the waving ladies to get their impression of Mr. Buttercup. One lady was blonde and the other brunette and they both looked very comfortable and settled in their loungers. They were very tan from spending their days at the pool. I think their "reserved" chaises were permanently dimpled with their impressions.

"Is that man with you ladies?" I asked them.

They looked at each other and giggled a little like schoolgirls.

"Oh no, he's a bit of a lothario here. He likes to flirt with all the ladies."

"He's really harmless, but it's fun to be pursued, like a schoolgirl again. He's always so attentive; he puts sunscreen on everyone and talks pretty to them," the blonde said.

"Oh, so he doesn't go out with just one lady at a time then?" Private Eyes asked.

"He may, I'm not sure. I always see him around a lot of ladies. It's all in fun. He pays attention to us and we flirt with him a little," the brunette lady said.

"Well, he did have a thing for Willow, though," the blonde lady countered. "She tried to monopolize him. She liked the attention, but she had eyes for the younger guys."

"Oh, I thought they dated. I heard he caused a jealous scene when he saw Willow with a young man at a dance," I prompted.

Both women unexpectedly burst out in laughter.

"I remember him. That young man was something to look at with hair slicked back, shirt wide open, and those tight pants. You could almost tell what religion he was." They both laughed.

"I guess he was a little hurt. She did lead him on, but he's a lover, not a fighter," the blonde lady said.

"So there wasn't a fight?" Private Eyes asked.

Both women let out big booming laughs again.

"Hardly a fight. He said something to them and then went away fuming," the brunette lady said.

We stayed and chatted a bit more about people and things in the community, so our questions would not seem out of place and arouse any suspicion, and then we left.

"Strike two on the gossip rumors. No fight, no threat and no suspect. Dead end," Private Eyes said.

I thought there was still something missing in that whole exchange. The ladies were very happy to dismiss it all as a joke, but they did say Binny was hurt and left angry. We needed to talk to Binny, but when I looked up, he was gone.

Neither Private Eyes nor I knew him personally, and luckily the ladies mentioned his real name, so we looked him up in the community directory and went to his home to ask him a few questions. We needed to find out his actual feelings for Willow.

We decided we need a cover story to explain why we were asking him questions, so we told him we were on the dance committee and wanted to discuss the altercation with the young man with him personally to get his side of the story.

He was quiet, and he graciously invited us into his home. It didn't look like a bachelor pad. In fact, it looked like it popped right out of the pages of *Martha Stewart Living*. Everything was neat and beautifully decorated.

The furniture was tasteful and somewhat modern. The colors were light and airy. Each picture frame and knickknack was deliberately poised on curios, shelves and side tables draped in fabric runners.

"We wanted to ensure that this type of thing doesn't happen anymore and we are considering restricting outside guests at these dances to protect residents," I said, positioning him to elicit a true response.

"I don't think anything that drastic is necessary," he said calmly. I know I shouldn't have approached him, but I thought they were acting a little risqué. I mean, it was pitiful. He was slobbering all over her on the dance floor. I don't mean to be indelicate in front of you ladies, but you could see tongues and everything. It was very improper," he said firmly.

"I can understand that—yuck," Private Eyes agreed.

"To be honest, I was worried about Willow. And that young man was obviously taking advantage of her."

"So you weren't jealous?" Private Eyes asked.

He let out a little chuckle and smiled awkwardly. "I am almost embarrassed to admit it, but I am a little sweet on Willow. She reminds me of my ex-wife. She was a take-charge kind of woman too. But I could see she was taken in by that—I hate to say it—dubious young man with his disco outfit and bad-boy good looks. Women like danger, not an evening of television and jigsaw puzzles with old me," he said with a forced grin.

"Why do you think he was taking advantage of her?" I asked to follow up on his assertion of danger.

"I don't think—I know!" he exclaimed, instantly perking up in his chair. "He's only interested in her for her money."

"Money?" Private Eyes and I asked together.

"Yes, I saw her give him money on many occasions. And I know others who saw them together at the restaurant and said she always paid for drinks and dinner. He's sponging off of her," he insisted.

"Why do you think she's wealthy?" I asked.

"She told me her aunt died and left her a fortune," he said.

We thanked him and politely left with some answers but more questions.

Binny was definitely interested in Willow, but genuinely seemed concerned about her. The young gigolo could be a clue. Both Binny and the ladies were sure he wasn't interested in Willow for her dancing or kissing abilities, but for her bankroll. The inheritance angle was new and required more investigation. I needed to report everything to Madame. Maybe the others came up with something more.

"You did great," I told Private Eyes. "You're very intuitive and fast on your feet. You'll fit right into our inquisitive group."

I left Private Eyes, but before I went home, I stopped by the lounge area to see Madame. She was often there, plopped in her favorite high-backed chair in the corner, where she could cloak herself and see and hear everything. She pretended to read a book, when really she was listening in on everyone's conversations and making notes. She was the ultimate community busybody.

I reported our lack of suspects at the pool and bar and mentioned the idea of the young gigolo as a possible suspect.

"In light of what we now believe is a wealthy Willow, money could be a clear motive," I said.

"Yes, the young gigolo boyfriend is already on our radar. Another team is looking into him. He was mentioned in some other footage about an argument between him and Willow in her home, she said.

As I drove my golf cart home, I was still puzzled. Willow obviously liked young men from her actions with Buck and this gigolo. And she may have strung Binny along just for the attention, but if money was the motive, why would a young gigolo want to get rid of her when he had a sugar mama to pay for everything?

When I got home, I had an email from Cluist with an article discussing possible death by poisoning.

Cluist said poison can be untraceable in some cases and can be administered slowly or quickly, depending on dosage. It said large dosages usually result in an immediate and spectacular death, but slow poisoning is the crime of familiarity, as small amounts are consumed regularly. So, if someone was around a victim all the time and knew their everyday movements, it would be easy to conceal the crime as an illness.

So it could be a measured poisoning resulting in a slow death. If we had a body, tests could be done to confirm poising or not, but we didn't have that option. Or maybe we did… maybe she just passed in her condo?

Chapter 3

The Condominium:

Captain Cluemaster

Daring Detective just called me about her poison theory, with the young gigolo as her main suspect.

We needed a tactical plan. After thirty years in the Army and the last fifteen with the military police, I dealt with my share of domestic issues. Sometimes when a soldier was gone a lot, rifts and resentments occurred with spouses.

I was not really one to jump to conclusions, but poison could be an option in this case. I had some experience in that arena.

One time, there was a soldier whose wife poisoned him very slowly, which made him constantly sick. He was stationed stateside then, but after years of being away from her, the damage was done. She hated him.

He was convinced he had cancer, but didn't tell anyone because he didn't want to get mustered out of the service.

But what she didn't know was that he secretly fed their three cats' food from his plate. When they all died one by one within two weeks, he became suspicious and called us.

We had their garbage tested and found poison in the food. He lived and she went to jail. That was some good detective work.

I'm glad to have a case to work on again. I'm used to being active, so after retirement, I filled my days with tennis, pickleball, ping pong and billiards clubs, but nothing gave me that adrenaline thrill I used to get in the Army. I tried mystery novels, but they just didn't quench my thirst like the real thing.

That's why I joined the sleuths club—to get my hands dirty again. Now I need to meet with the team and go over the gossip. I find chitchat to be useless in most cases, but it's what we have to work with. In the Army, we had a saying, improvise, adapt and overcome.

"Everyone, listen up. We have a few leads from our gossip trail, but there are a lot of assumptions. The first camera footage involved several neighbors at the Parrot condos talking about our missing person. Madame named it… uh… *Happy Hijinks*." I said.

A: You live in the Parrot condo neighborhood, don't you?

B: Yes.

A: Do you know Willow Wisteria?

B: We wave to each other. She lives on the other end of my floor, but I can't say I really know her. Why are you asking?

A: Well, you know I hate to gossip, but someone in my exercise class says she got a package of Willow's by mistake. And it was from Happy Endings Massage Company in New York.

C: Did you say Happy Endings?

A: Yes. And I think Willow is from New York.

B: She does get a lot of packages. I just saw a huge stack outside her door. Some did have the word "Intimate" on them.

C: Intimate? What could that be?

B: Maybe she's into massage therapy.

A: I don't know what she's into, but a lot of people are talking about that woman.

C: That's true. She's single and you always see her with different men at the pool and even at the dances.

B: Come on, I think you are letting your imagination go wild here. Maybe she runs a massage business out of her home. There's nothing wrong with that.

C: Is she giving happy endings?

A: Maybe the name on the boxes is a dodge to throw people off? I saw this movie once where they hid drugs in boxes marked "coffee" so no one would suspect. Maybe they aren't intimates, but they could be drugs or something else illegal.

B: I saw that movie too. They were smuggling bearer bonds, precious gems and artwork into the country too.

C: I don't know if someone could really do that in real life—that seems a little far-fetched.

"I wouldn't get a happy ending from that woman," Master Mayhem laughed.

"Ok, well, that may be true, but unless you killed her, it's irrelevant. Let's keep our eye on the ball, people. The next footage was a little more revealing, as it involved several neighbors who talked about a supposed argument between our MIA and a potential suspect. This one was called *Garbage Gripes*. Madame and her stupid names," I said.

A: Hey, have you seen Willow around recently? These packages are stacking up outside her door.

B: No, the last time I saw her was a couple of weeks ago. She and (Petunia Periwinkle) were having a big fight about the trash chute.

C: Oh, because she stuffs it with all her boxes?

B: Right, everybody in the building knows it's her. She always clogs the chute up so everyone has to go to the bottom floor to get rid of their garbage. Every day poor (Petunia) spends nearly an hour pushing the boxes down with her broom so they can go into the incinerator. That's a lot of work on the arms.

A: I know the association sent Willow letters about that. She must just ignore them.

B: Well, (Petunia) was pushing the boxes down when Willow came with more. She just snapped and said, "You tosser, quit plugging up the bloody trash chute." Then Willow got mad and said, "What are you calling me?" Then (Petunia) said, "Well, any idiot knows you can't cook ten quarts of mash in a five-quart pot. So I guess I am calling you an idiot." I thought there was going to be a fight until someone came along and they stopped. And (Petunia) was so mad, she yelled, "Maybe someone should stuff you into the chute!"

A: Wow, she must have been upset.

C: Now that you mention it, I just got an email from the association about the incinerator. They told everyone to make sure everything was in bags going into the trash chute. One of the board members told me they keep finding objects lying next to the incinerator. He said a couple of weeks ago they even found a red shoe with flowers all over it next to the incinerator.

A: Wait, a red shoe with flowers all over it? Willow has shoes like that. She wears them all the time.

C: She does? No, you don't think?

"I know Petunia—she wouldn't do anything like that." Mystery Minx stood up and folded her arms.

"Look, you heard Madame, everyone is guilty unless proven innocent," I said. "Let's just get through this last video and we can discuss. This one showed another group of neighbors at the Parrot condos in front of the mailboxes. There were a lot of discussions at this condo. This one was called *Condo Caper*."

A: Did you hear Willow Wisteria disappeared?

B: What? No, she must just be visiting someone.

A: No, she missed our card game yesterday and I haven't seen her in over a week. And someone on the Nosy Neighbors app was asking if anyone saw her.

B: Well, I did notice a huge stack of packages the other day and then I just walked by there today and there were more. It didn't look like they had been picked up.

C: Come to think of it, she wasn't at pickleball today either.

A: See, there's something fishy about this. I play tennis with her downstairs neighbor and the neighbor said she's always hearing weird noises coming from Willow's condo.

C: Like what?

A: Well, recently she heard Willow arguing with a man and then she said it sounded like furniture being moved around.

B: Furniture? I wonder if Willow was arguing with her boyfriend.

A: You mean boyfriends. My friend said she sees men coming down the stairs from her place all the time.

B: Yes, I've heard that too.

C: I hate to say this, but has anyone seen her leave the condo? Could she be in there?

A: Maybe. She lives alone—she could be dead in there for weeks and no one would know.

"Oh no, that poor woman could be rotting away in there," Minx said.

"Don't worry, with all the hooch she reportedly drank, that woman is naturally embalmed," laughed Mayhem and Minx hit him with her dossier folder.

"I agree. If she is hurt or dead in the condo, I don't think we have any choice but to get inside. The end must justify the means. Let's unpack all this and make a plan of attack. Getting into that condo is our first target. And Daring Detective's team floated a theory about poison with one of the boyfriends as a suspect," I said.

"The neighbor in that video said she heard an argument with a man, so that could be true," Mayhem said.

"Well, I don't believe Petunia Periwinkle would hurt a flea, but she is in my pinochle group and I have heard her complain about those boxes in the trash chute. I'll talk to her," Minx added.

"Since all the homes have electronic locks, I think we can use a liquid chemical solution to see what keys were pressed on the keypad. I saw it in a movie. I'll talk to Chemical Cluist; I bet he can figure out something," Mayhem said.

"Ok, I'm going to see if I can find out what was in those boxes. Let me know if you can get into her condo so we can investigate," I ordered, and then dismissed everyone so I could think.

Captain Cluemaster

We had to know what Willow was up to, so I went to her condo, hoping to find some boxes stacked outside her door.

From the gossip in the video, I thought there would be huge stacks of boxes, but there was one stack; a typical exaggeration. I picked up a couple, just to take a look, but I was interrupted red-handed in my attempt.

"Do you know Willow? Are you one of her man friends?" a neighbor accused.

She looked a lot like one of the neighbors in the videos.

"No, I am not one of her man friends. I have the same unit number in the building across the street. The Amazon guy sometimes gets our packages mixed up. This is one of hers and I wanted to see if she had one of mine. The app said it was delivered today."

"The last thing she needs is more packages. UPS, Amazon and the post office are all here twice a day to deliver stuff to her," she ranted.

"That is a lot. Did she ever tell you what she has delivered?"

"Ha, not me. I've complained to the association about all her deliveries and the constant stream of men coming in and out of this place day and night," she continued.

"Oh, do they make a lot of noise?"

"Well, yes and no. Usually they are playing music into the late hours. It's usually like Sodom and Gomorrah, but lately it's been quiet," she said.

"Oh really, when was the last time you heard the music?"

The elevator binged, and she walked toward the doors.

"About two weeks ago. I've got to go. Hope you find your package," she said. The elevator doors opened and she left abruptly.

So, sounds like two weeks ago could be the accurate timeline. This time, I looked around the hallway for anyone else. I'm slipping in my old age. I would have never been caught before. Seeing no one, I grabbed a few packages and quickly moved to my car to open them.

Just as the intel footage suggested, the packages were addressed from Happy Endings Massage Company in New York. I was almost afraid to open them. With all the scuttlebutt, I wasn't really in the mood to see a lot of "S&M" stuff.

I opened each box and held my breath. Two had bottles labeled scented lotions and essential oils. They had very odd names like "Beach Bounty," "Luscious Lavender," "Glorious Glide," "Salacious Sandalwood," "Natural Nutty" and "Premium Pepper." But then again, I'm old school. I only use old-fashioned generic petroleum jelly on rashes and itches.

Another box contained some of those hot rocks used in massage. So far, the massage rumor checked out. With these tools, it looked legitimate. But the last one had the strangest contraption. It was a tube with a hand pump like a blood-pressure cuff. There was a booklet under it entitled "The Enlarger."

I quickly closed it up. I didn't want to read anymore. Even after years cooped up with men in the Army, I guess I could still get embarrassed by some things.

Maybe the gossip was right. Maybe she was giving "happy endings" to men. I needed more info, but there was definitely something strange going on in that condo. We had to get in there.

Mystery Minx

I wanted to handle Petunia myself so I could clear her name. She's my neighbor. When I first came into this community, she was my guide. I was recently widowed and basically starting my life all over again. I had no one and no idea how to begin. She instantly befriended me, got me into her pinochle club, and introduced me to people in the community. I made friends, and it started me out on my new journey. I owed her.

She could not have killed Willow. That was preposterous. She's eighty years old, frail and less than five feet tall. She could barely kill a spider—certainly not a person. I was determined to clear her name, but I still needed to act like a professional detective. I couldn't give too much away.

"Hello, are you home?" I knocked on her screen. She always kept her door wide open and her screen unlocked. She said she liked the breeze.

"Oh, hello, dear. Come on in. I'm in the kitchen making tea," she said.

It was teatime. Petunia was a petite sweet English lady with gray hair, very pale skin and a bit of a hunch, as she walked with a cane. She'd been here in the U.S. for many years, but she still had links to jolly old England. She even had a picture of Queen Elizabeth on the wall. Now that I look at Petunia and the queen together, they actually look alike.

One of her honored traditions was her daily tea, with a wonderful spread of homemade scones with clotted cream and preserves. Even if she was alone, she laid out her delicate bone china set and flowered linens on the kitchen table for afternoon high tea.

"You're just in time for high tea, dear," she said, pouring a cup into the gold flowered tea setting.

"Lucky I came by." I sat down, sipped tea, and talked to her about the weather and other trivial conversation starters, trying to figure out how to ask her about Willow.

"There's been a lot of talk about the argument you had with Willow Wisteria," I blurted out.

"Oh, you mean over those bloody boxes? I admit I got my ire up at her. It's hard for me to take my trash all the way down to the incinerator, with my cane and all. Her boxes kept stopping up the chute, so I pushed them down with a broom, but it hurt my arm and my back. That day I had enough and when she came with more boxes, I admit I lost my temper," she explained.

"Did you threaten her?" I asked.

She paused for the longest time and then let out a little giggle.

"You know, I may have. I'm just not sure. I can sometimes say things in the heat of the moment, you know. I have my Irish grandmother's temper sometimes."

She kept drinking her tea and eating her scone. Her giggle reaction was surprising, but still seemed innocent.

"Well, you understand why it's suspicious given all the talk about Willow?" I asked.

"You know I don't engage in gossip, dear. What has she done now?" she asked in an uncharacteristically sarcastic tone.

"She's missing and there's talk of foul play," I said bluntly.

"Oh, fiddlesticks!" she yelled as she abruptly dropped her scone on the plate and quietly looked down.

"What do you know about this?" I asked her curiously.

"Now, you know I don't tell tales out of the yard, but I did overhear an odd conversation between Willow and a man a few weeks back. They knew each other, and she was plenty cheesed at him. She was squawking like a parrot. I didn't hear what they were talking about. But I did hear her loudly say she didn't want to go with him."

"And you didn't report this to anyone?" I asked.

"No. Oh, dear. She's always so unpleasant. I've heard her in a tizzy many times with everyone. It didn't even occur to me it might have been dodgy."

She genuinely looked worried. She sat there still, looking out into space, not even drinking her tea. I was confused. I thought her concern was over a potential abduction and not making good on her threat, but I needed to probe further.

"So… you didn't stuff her down the trash chute, right?" I blurted out.

She looked at me with a peculiar stare that I'd never seen on her face before.

"Is that what people are saying? Oh my, I was just having a row with her. How would tiny me stuff a grown woman into a trash chute that doesn't even fit her boxes? It's a lot of nonsense, that is." She shook her head and awkwardly laughed a little.

"Yes, it is silly. That's why I wanted to tell you," I said. "But I'm glad you told me about the man. Sounds like she didn't want to go with him?"

She sighed and looked down again. "She was cheesed, but she didn't scream or anything. It never even crossed my mind that she was in danger."

"Don't worry about it. I'm sure it was nothing," I said to comfort her and drank my tea.

I stayed for a little bit and finished the tea. I was sure Petunia was innocent, but I wasn't certain she didn't accidentally overhear an abduction.

Captain Cluemaster

The next day I met with the team and Chemical Cluist at the condo to open the door. Cluist came up with a special florescent solution that would make the fingerprints on the keypad show up under black light. Since all the locks in the community used a four-digit combination, if we could see the numbers pressed, by process of elimination, we could figure out the code. I was unnerved by how easy it was to access the keypad.

We went at night to avoid prying eyes and assist with the darkness for the black light. I came equipped with my set of night vision goggles, like I had in the Army. They were always helpful for stealth work.

I had everyone on the team there for mutual protection; after all, we were breaking and entering. And we would need a lot of hands to look for clues. Plus, if there was a dead body in there, I didn't want to be the only one to find it. It's not that I was squeamish; I just didn't want to deal with it alone.

"I did some research," Mayhem explained. "There are ten thousand possible combinations that the digits 0-9 can be arranged to form a four-digit code. I checked with the manufacturer of the locks and these locks will not accept duplicate digits, and since we know they are four digits, that left us with twenty-four possible permutations. Maybe we'll get lucky."

"And there you go—science to the rescue." Cluist shined a black light on the small keypad to reveal the four luminescent numbers used.

"My research also said a code is usually something obvious or something personal. I checked our resident database and I have her birth date, birth year and phone number. But these four numbers eliminate her birth date, birth year and the last four digits of her phone number. I'll try one of the common codes I found." Master Mayhem started entering combinations on the keypad.

Minx looked at the paper with her personal information. "Actually, try her birth date again. If you take her birth month and subtract five years from her birth year that could work. People lie about their age all the time in the directory, but she would use her real birth year as the combo."

"Aha! You did it—it's open!" Mayhem gleamed excitedly.

Mayhem opened the door into the black abyss and we all stood there. We came there to find out, but faced with reality, no one rushed in to be the first to find a dead body. I had to break the silence; after all, we were safer inside.

"Ok. Does everyone have gloves on? Just in case this becomes a police investigation, we shouldn't leave any fingerprints. And don't use that black light on anything else, Cluist. There are some things I don't want to know."

Everyone responded with empty mechanical nods of approval.

I proceeded into the dark condo first, with the others close behind. The others had flashlights, as we wanted to limit the lights to avoid the suspicion of the neighbors.

I could see everything with my goggles and stayed ahead of their flashlights so they didn't blind me. One room at a time, we searched the two-bedroom condo for a body and eliminated each room with a sigh of relief. With all the main areas clean, we split up to search more thoroughly.

I was alone in the master bedroom, looking in the closets. I feared I'd be the one to find something. And I did. In the master walk-in closet, I saw a figure lying lifelessly on the floor.

Despite overwhelming dread, I recalled my training and pulled off the bandage quickly. So, I took off my night vision goggles and turned on the closet light. There it was—a fabric-covered, life-sized dummy with a blonde wig. I was relieved. If she was a masseuse, this might be a practice dummy.

After searching the home and finding no dead body, we now were on the hunt for clues. We closed the blinds and curtains and turned on the lights to recon one room at a time.

The condo was typical for the area. It had light-colored walls and a beachy feel with comfortable furniture. One strange thing was, it seemed a little impersonal, like a hotel room. It didn't have any personal touches, like framed pictures of family and friends or even those chachkies my wife lines every surface of our home with. It was clean, but very impersonal.

I briefed the team on what I found in the boxes and collected the rest of the boxes to investigate inside the condo. With the lotions, oils and other items I found in the boxes, plus the dummy in the closet, the masseuse rumor was still a distinct possibility.

First, we opened all the boxes. We found more essential oils, towels that looked like shammies, Egyptian cotton sheets and some other items.

"Uh, you guys better look at this." Minx stepped away from a box and looked away.

"How about that? Fun in a box!" Mayhem laughed and pulled out various sex toys from the box, holding them up.

"Here's another box full of them. She was amassing quite a collection." Cluist and Mayhem laughed again.

"I think we can eliminate the smuggling theory, but given all these 'therapy items,' I think we can assume Willow was the adventurous type and potentially was giving massages with 'happy endings,'" I said.

"Maybe a jealous wife did her in?" Mayhem quipped.

We looked through the rest of the condo again, room by room, looking in drawers and closets. There was still some clothing in the closets and in some drawers, but other drawers were empty.

"I don't see a computer anywhere, but some people this age don't have one," Cluist said. "I need to check the silverware, plates and cups to see if I can get any poison residue. It's a long shot, but I have a solution that can detect chemicals."

"I know, to save time, why not put them all in the dishwasher and let the solution run over them?" Mayhem offered.

"Thanks, but that's too much water; then they would be too clean. I need to do this by hand," Cluist answered.

"I found some makeup in this bath drawer, but not much. Maybe she didn't use a lot." Minx closed the bath drawers. "I don't know many women who would leave for anywhere without their makeup."

"How did the talk with Petunia go?" I asked Minx.

"She did have words with Willow over the boxes. She didn't remember what was said for sure, but she admitted she could have said someone should put her in the trash chute in the heat of the moment," Minx said.

"Well, that's it, the old lady went bonkers and put her in the incinerator. They found Willow's stuff near the incinerator. She's guilty. Case closed," Mayhem said.

"No!" Minx objected. "That doesn't make any sense. Petunia is a small little old lady… with a cane. She couldn't lift her into the incinerator and Willow wouldn't go easily. And the trash chute gets clogged by boxes, so how could a whole person go into it? But she also told me she overheard Willow arguing with a man in front of her condo a few weeks ago. Petunia heard Willow say she didn't want to go with him."

"She didn't see who it was or recognize the voice?" I asked.

"No, she didn't think it was anything at the time. She said Willow didn't scream; she just seemed mad at the guy," Minx explained.

"Maybe it was the boyfriend? In the camera footage the other neighbor did report that fight she overheard and furniture moving," Mayhem added.

"Yes, that is one theory. The neighbor I spoke with earlier said something similar about arguments and a lot of parties and noise with men. Ok, I guess we can eliminate the incinerator speculation and Petunia, but we need to consider the boyfriend, whoever he is, under suspicion." I agreed.

"Or boyfriends. There were men coming in and out of here all the time, according to the neighbors. How are we going to trace them?" Mayhem asked.

Chapter 4

Arts and Crafts:

Magnolia Mastermind

I was more excited than a bunch of bees on the first spring blooming day. I felt like I was an honest to goodness detective. I've always been a curious person, like that Curious George in the picture books. Even as a little bitty sprout growing up in Georgia, I had a desperate need to know everything all the time. I listened to adult conversations in church, at the store and in my parents' house. I love me some juicy gossip.

As a young debutante, I found I didn't look for the tittle-tattle; it came right to me. All my life, I've been the keeper of all the secrets and I loved it. For some reason, people felt comfortable telling me all their worries and woes. It was that genteel upbringing and charm we in the South are known for.

Sparks and Newshound were off doing their own thing, so Delta Snoops and I decided to go it alone. And since it dealt with some doings in the arts and crafts room, we were the perfect ones to investigate. We Southern belles were in those rooms all the time on account of how we loved making pretty things.

I was working on a beautiful vase to use for my flowers. I loved the smell of fresh flowers. It gave you a wonderful sense of being and frankly reminded me of my old Georgia home. That's why I made my detective name Magnolia. That was before Madame decided to use flower names for all the suspects, but I'm not changing my name.

"Delta, this video, you'll have to excuse the language, was named *P****d Off About Pots,*" *I said.*

A: Come on, we'll be late for pottery class and we won't get to the kiln before Willow.

B: Willow? Didn't you hear? She hasn't shown up for class in weeks. Everyone's talking about it.

C: No, I was just in the arts room the other day finishing up a project with (Iris Impatiens) and she said Willow left her pot in the kiln overnight. She said they were walking in the butterfly garden and lost track of time.

A: No, she's right; there are rumors all around the perch about Willow. But I heard their argument was because (Iris) found out Willow was stealing supplies from the craft room.

B: I have no problem believing that, but Willow wouldn't walk with (Iris). They hate each other. In fact, a couple of weeks ago, they had a screaming match in pottery class over that kiln. Willow took (Iris's) pot out of the kiln to put hers in and it wasn't done, so it caved in. Iris was furious.

A: Then why would they go to the butterfly garden together? Maybe it was before the kiln incident?

B: Oh, it must have been, but I think I did see them. I was walking my dog and saw (Iris) taking Willow's picture on the bridge.

C: That bridge scares me; it's right over that creek that they find the alligators in all the time.

A: You don't think she fell in and was eaten by alligators, do you?

C: Or pushed in?

B: That's silly. No one kills someone over pottery. Let's get to class.

"Well, Miss Iris seems to be a heap of a mess," I said. "She could be a suspect."

"That's plum crazy; Iris is not the killing kind," Delta said. "Plus, who would be dang fool enough to kill someone for a pot? I don't believe it." She folded her arms and shook her head back and forth in determined defiance.

"Now then, if you're right, we need to prove Iris innocent beyond a shadow of a doubt. It's open project time now in the crafts room. Let's go see what we can find out, I said.

Our crafts room was done all in white, like a blank canvas. It was very functional for many different kinds of art, with tables and cabinets for all the supplies. They recently installed cubbies all around the room so everyone could store their works-in-progress for safekeeping. That quelled some of the fights, but now the biggest arguments were over supplies and the kiln.

There was only one kiln. It was big enough for a few projects at a time, but people tend to be a little territorial now and then.

Luckily, Delta and I both had projects in progress, so we pretended we were working while gently making inquiries. And the best of luck was, Iris was not in the room, but there were three other ladies working on their projects.

We were going to make believe we heard the rumors and let the tittle-tattle naturally flow.

"See Delta, you didn't leave your pot in the kiln overnight; it's right here in your cubby, you silly," I said.

We walked into the room and started our ruse.

"Oh, I'm so glad. Remember the last time someone left a pot in the kiln and someone else took it out? It was ruined," Delta pretended.

"I know exactly what you're talking about," one lady said. "There was a big fight over that a few weeks ago. I wasn't in the room, mind you, but everyone's been talking about it. They came to blows."

"Oh my, a fistfight? How unladylike," I added.

"Don't spread rumors—there was no fistfight," the second lady rebutted. "I heard the lady found her ruined pot on the counter and Willow's pot in the kiln, so she smashed both pots on the ground in a rage."

"Do tell—she really smashed her pot to bits?" Delta chimed in.

"Just STOP! People shouldn't open their mouths if they weren't there. I WAS there and I saw everything," a third lady told. "There were no fisticuffs. And no one smashed any pots. I mean, really, how do these rumors start? She found her pot on the counter ruined and suspected it was Willow, since her name was the next name on the kiln sign-in sheet. She was mad and did say some nasty things about Willow, but that was that," the third lady said.

"Maybe, but she talked to my friend, and she said she had it with Willow," the first lady said. "Remember she caught her stealing community art supplies."

"That was never proven!" The third lady said with her voiced raised.

"Maybe not, but everyone saw the glass beads on Willow's pot. They were in the cabinet before she was in the room, alone, and they were gone afterward. You do the math, detective," the second lady shouted.

"My, my, ladies, I do believe it's getting a little heated in here," I prodded a little more. "We have all heard of Willow's notorious misdeeds."

"And some even say Iris had something to do with Willow's disappearing act," Delta added to get a reaction.

"No, no," the ladies objected in a synchronous chorus.

"That's ridiculous; no one would harm someone over a pot," the first lady insisted.

"Well, I just wondered because someone said they two were seen walking together to the bridge a few weeks ago," Delta said, waiting for the answer.

"They did?" the ladies asked in concert.

"That's strange," the first lady said with a big-eyed look on her face.

"It's just a dumb rumor," the second lady said slowly and softly with her head down on her project.

After a disturbing silence of nearly five minutes, the third lady spoke up again.

"I just don't believe anyone would do anything like that."

It was a like a tennis match. This one believed this and that one heard that. Who knew what to believe? And they were all so fervent in their stories and arguments, even though some didn't exactly witness it. People were funny sometimes, but usually very predictable; they will always talk. With the chitchat done, Delta and I finished up and made our excuses to leave the room.

"I think there is a glimmer of doubt. They were so adamant at Iris's innocence at first, but then they were not so sure. I think we need to check out that bridge area," Delta said.

I agreed, so Delta and I walked down to the old bridge.

The bridge used to be part of the walking path to the butterfly garden, but it started to become dangerous, so they made a new path to the butterfly garden. I loved butterflies; it felt so natural in the garden with them buzzing all around.

The wood on the bridge was in simply horrible disrepair and was going to take a lot of money to replace. Plus, the creek underneath became a breeding ground for the alligators in the neighborhood ponds to lay their eggs and care for their young.

The residents went there to take pictures of the baby alligators. There were snapshots of them posted constantly with everyone "ooohing" and "ahhing" over the baby alligators, like they were looking through the glass at newborn human babies in a maternity ward. And they even fed the baby alligators and some named the mother Ali and gave cute little names to all the babies.

I thought it was silly nonsense to play den mother to them. Little baby alligators turned into big dangerous alligators and there was nothing cute about that. I believe in live and let live, but I'm not asking for trouble.

The managers told everyone the bridge was unstable and posted signs, but people didn't listen. Someone nearly fell in trying to take a picture of the babies when part of the bridge railing came down. Then the managers blocked it off with red "danger" tape. I shuddered to think of what could've happened if someone fell in with mama alligator trying to protect her young'uns.

When we arrived, one whole railing on the bridge was gone. I didn't know if management took it down or if it collapsed; although we saw some random pieces of wood on the banks around the creek.

"See, that railing collapsed and someone may have fallen in… or been pushed in," Delta said.

"There are not enough pieces on the ground to make up for a whole railing," I refuted.

"Maybe the rest fell in the water and went upstream," Delta proposed.

Delta and I carefully looked around, staying on the banks. I found a red golf visor, like a lot of women wear, and near that, we found a cellphone with a red floral case. It was dead, cracked and waterlogged, like it washed up on the shore.

"That's it—Iris did it. She pushed Willow in and the alligator ate her body," Delta said confidently. "Call Madame and tell her."

"This does look awful suspicious, but that's a mighty big jump. We don't know this is Willow's phone. I'll get this evidence to Madame. Maybe some tech-savvy person can resuscitate this device," I countered.

I couldn't help but draw the same conclusion. Iris was known to have a beastly temper. But would she really carry out this ghastly offense?

Delta had to go, as bingo was about to start and she wanted to get there early to get a good seat, so we both walked back to the recreation center.

I wasn't able to shake the nagging feeling that we could have a murderer among us in our friendly little community. It gave me the chills. So, instead of going to talk to Madame, I decided to see if I could find Iris. I truly believed that everyone should have their day in court to speak their mind. If she was guilty, I thought I would know. Like I said before, people talked to me.

I went back to the arts and crafts room first. Rumor had it that she was often in there, as she was kind-of the self-imposed boss of the room. There she was, all alone. Iris looked like shot-putter in the Olympics. She was broad-shouldered and a little intimidating, especially with her gruff, direct manner of speech.

"As I live and breathe, I am so glad I caught you—I mean, found you," I said, tripping over my words when I found Iris alone in the room.

"I have a question about my project. You are such an expert at this. How tall do you think I can make this vase? I don't want it collapsing in the kiln like a sunken soufflé," I asked.

"Well, the height doesn't really matter. It just depends how long it is in the kiln," she said curtly, barely looking up.

She was working on a bowl. I sat across from her and pretended to work on mine.

"Oh yes, I heard something in the wind about a pot that was ruined because it wasn't in the kiln long enough."

I innocently poked at her, but she just sighed and growled a little and kept working on her pot. I needed to go a little further.

"Hmm… where did I hear that? Oh yes, some ladies told me someone else took it out too early. I don't know about you, but that's just not neighborly," I said.

"Exactly! That was my pot, and I worked a long time on it. People have no consideration for others these days. All they care about is themselves."

Iris wasn't mad, but she wasn't calm either. I was not proud of myself, but I knew I had to push some buttons, gently, to get her to crack.

"You are speaking the very gospel sister. We all need to share this equipment fairly. As the Good Book says, do unto others. I think that person should have their privileges taken away as punishment to teach them some manners," I said.

Suddenly, Iris got a strange look on her face with big bright eyes and a twisted smile peeking at the edge of her face. Honestly, it looked a mite sinister. Maybe I was getting to her.

"I see you agree. I hate to be harsh, but sometimes people won't behave unless they are taught a lesson. Just like children," I said defiantly, and then waited for her response.

"Yes. The message was sent to her loud and clear." She smiled and was oddly silent for a few minutes.

Now I was a little scared. Maybe she did the deed. Was I sitting next to a cool, calculating murderess?

"I complained to the manager, and they sent her a letter of suspension for a week from the pottery room. That'll show her," she explained without looking up.

"Oh, that's why I haven't seen her. Can you believe there's a silly little old rumor about her falling off that rickety bridge? I don't know what anyone was doing out there, anyway," I nudged her a little.

"That's not a rumor. I was out there with her. Once she got the letter, she apologized and asked me to retract my complaint. I told her she had to do me a favor. I wanted to get a picture of me with Ali's babies. I've been watching those cute little ones closely. I know it's silly, but it's an affirmation in a new life being born. So she went out there with me and got on the bridge to get a good photo. But she didn't fall," she clarified in a very matter-of-fact tone.

She showed me the picture taken at the bridge. Of course, all you could see were her and the baby alligators. Anyone could have taken it.

"So she left there safe and sound?" I asked.

"Well, I don't really know. She took the picture with my phone and then I left. She got a text as we were leaving and she said she needed to deal with it. I didn't see her after that," Iris said.

I excused myself and left. She admitted to being with Willow at the bridge, but claims she was unharmed when she left her. That seemed very convenient. I was even more confused and my head hurt. I needed to take an aspirin and lie down for a while. I'll report to Madame in the morning.

Chapter 5

The Roundup:

Madame Sleuth

The investigation was coming along well! I was to be congratulated for gathering such a superior sleuths society together. We had several suspects and some tantalizing theories so far. I thought I should meet with the society to go over our findings, as some of these fascinating facts overlap in the investigations, so they could all have the benefit of my wisdom and wit.

"I've gathered you to round up the information so far. Some of you have been talking to each other, but I would prefer to continue to be a conduit and clearing house for all clues," I directed. "Daring Detective, what has your team uncovered?"

"As far as suspects are concerned, we eliminated the bartender for lack of motive. We think he was just a pawn

Willow was toying with, just like Mr. Buttercup. His potential motive of jealousy is a bit shaky, but doesn't seem to be a crime of passion. And we added an unknown young man to the suspect list who has been seen in Willow's company."

"Yes, through decisive deductions, we have several other suspects who are still being examined. Their motives and their relationships to our victim are still unknown," I said.

"And Binny Buttercup claimed that Willow inherited a lot of money, so that could be a motive, right?" Private Eyes blurted out.

"It fits nicely into a bow-wrapped box for his theory about her young man friend. Binny thought he was trying to swindle her, but we don't know enough about him yet," Daring added.

"We can scratch Petunia Periwinkle from the list too," Mystery Minx declared. "But she did hear an argument between a man and Willow and she said the man was trying to take her somewhere against her will. It could have been this 'boyfriend.'"

"Several neighbors at the condo heard her arguing with a man at different times, so there could be more than one man," said Cluemaster.

"Yes, more investigation is needed there. And Daring Detective's team is still toying with the means of murder as poison." I agreed.

"Yes, since no one saw her struggle or choke, it could have been a long-game poisoning from someone who was close or familiar to her," Cluist explained. "But I checked every plate, cup and piece of silverware in her condo and there was no trace of poison. That doesn't mean it wasn't poisoning. Any residue could have been rinsed off in the dishwasher. Poison can be put into anything. You don't have to ingest it. It can be something that seeps into the skin too."

"Very well. Let's stay on track. We will still consider poison as a means," I directed.

"Someone broke into her condo?" Inspector Instinct asked with concerned.

"Quite right. Captain Cluemaster and team have searched her condominium. Unfortunately, they found nobody but there were a few clues," I said.

"Yes, we were able to figure out the access code to her electronic lock. The condo was oddly lacking personal items, but there were still clothes in the closet and a number of boxes of lotions, essential oils, hot stones, and even some sex toys," Cluemaster laughed.

"Sex toys?!" Magnolia exclaimed. "Oh, my my. A neighbor told Delta that she thought Willow was running a brothel."

"A brothel?" Daring asked, surprised at the accusation.

"Well, that could be," said Cluemaster. "It's hard to explain away those tricks of the trade, so to speak."

"Maybe that young gigolo could be her employee?" Delta asked.

"Or maybe her pimp?" Magnolia asked.

"I think you mean *she* was *his* pimp." Smoking Gun sighed and corrected her naivete.

"Is anyone even concerned that now we have committed the crime of breaking and entering?" Inspector Instinct stood up and shouted.

"Actually, it was just entering as they did not break anything, since they used the code. And since they didn't steal or disturb anything, whether or not that is a crime is a gray area. Maybe just trespassing, which is a lesser crime," Smoking Gun calmly explained, while lighting his cigar.

"Ok, snooping around is one thing, but we can't go too far with this. It's just a hobby after all," Inspector Instinct sat down and quietly stated, removing his objection.

"Look, I told you all to remove your inhibitions or walk out the door. The end justifies the means. Investigation can get a little ruthless, but it is necessary," I responded. "Now, let's stay on point, people. Unsavory as it is, sex therapy, with whatever that entails, is one potential theory. Several neighbors reported men continually coming in and out of Willow's home. And one neighbor said she was giving him cash."

"It all makes sense, but could she make money from prostitution here?" Daring asked.

"Who knows, there are a lot of men here, single and married, who may have need of those… services," Delta added.

"I think they call that making it rain," Mayhem joked.

"Ahem-let's keep it professional, ladies and gentlemen. And Mayhem, please remember, you are a gentleman," I scolded him to keep everyone on track.

"Very well, then. We discovered some new posts on Mugbook and Nosy Neighbors about Willow. It seems speculation about Willow has recently increased.

Everybody's talking about Willow Wisteria.

About what?

No one has seen her in weeks.

One less cheater…

Good riddance, she's not a nice person

Grow up!

Really, people? I hope she's ok.

What if it were you or your friends?

She doesn't have any friends.

Love Thy Neighbor.

Has anyone heard anything about her? Or seen her?

I haven't seen her, but I've heard a lot of rumors about her.

Maybe she's with Jimmy Hoffa?

Don't you people have anything better to do with your time?

Put out a Silver Alert!

"Of course, no Silver Alert was issued by the police, as no one has reported her missing... yet. And we can disregard the Jimmy Hoffa quip, but it's obvious that she is indeed missing," I said.

"And no one has any concrete information, just insipid gossip," Inspector Instinct said.

"Maybe, but you never know what clues can be found by following the gossip trail," Smoking Gun said.

"I thought that was the money trail," Instinct quipped.

"Money often leads to the culprit, but in my experience, rumors can be like gold. You filter out the garbage and you can sometimes find something valuable," Smoking Gun corrected.

"Yes, that's true. On that point, Inspector Instinct is using his accounting skills and connections to delve into her finances and see what comes up. That'll tell if someone would be after her for her money."

"I'll check into her background. I can find out anything on anyone," Smoking Gun said.

"Excellent. Moving on, without a body, the means still eludes us. So, everything is still on the table," I added.

"If it was murder, don't you think someone would have found a body by now?" asked Daring Detective.

"Not necessarily; there are many places in this community to hide or even bury a body. Swamps, woods, ponds, even concrete in the houses they're still building," Smoking Gun added, followed by lingering stares from the others.

"However unseemly, that's true. Now then, everyone has their assignments. Time is running out. Eventually, someone will report her to the police and then we're out of the game. We need something concrete. We'll reconvene in three days' time."

Chapter 6

The New York Connection:

Inspector Instinct

I told everyone I used to be an accountant. It was just easier. Actually, I was a forensic accountant and auditor for the IRS. I found people recoiled from me when they understood I could know everything about each detail of their financial existence.

I tapped some of my old sources to check Willow's bank accounts and credit cards. Her domestic accounts didn't show anything particularly unusual. She had a direct deposit for Social Security credited to her account every month, which is normal.

Her credit cards were paid off every month, with no odd charges. Most of the expenses were to that Happy Endings Massage Company in New York.

The rest were typical charges at stores, beauty salons, restaurants and tickets for the theater and movies, but that could be true of anyone here. She seemed to entertain a lot. There were even a couple of entries for an arcade on the beach pier, but nothing out of the ordinary.

The only curiosities were the age and number of the accounts; none of them were more than a few years old. People changed banks and credit cards, but typically older people are creatures of habit and stayed with the same companies for a while. And she had five different bank accounts with very little balance in each, which is atypical.

Since there was a question of a large inheritance, I'm waiting to hear from some bank contacts I have in the Cayman Islands. Willow's domestic accounts showed she had no significant wealth, but she could have purchased her condo and car for cash.

The team will be here any minute to go over our camera footage. It was taken of a couple's conversation in the community restaurant. Madame called it *New York Nosch and News*.

A: I think I'll have the carbonara with clams and I definitely want cannoli for dessert. And let's get a bottle of Chianti.

B: I love coming here on Italian night. Feels just like home. I miss New York cuisine.

A: Already? We've only been here in Florida for a month.

B: A person can only have so much fish. I think I'll get the clams with linguini. Hey, did I tell you I thought I saw someone from the old neighborhood?

A: No, who?

B: That's the thing. She looked so familiar. I know I've seen her at family events before.

A: Do you mean family events or f-a-m-i-l-y events?

B: You know what I mean. I think she was a secretary; she was the one who was always in charge of the Christmas parties. Actually, maybe she worked for da boss. I remember, she always wore red dresses, but then again, it was at Christmas parties.

A: You saw HER here?

B: I think so. Her name started with a W—it was an unusual name. Not Italian. Anyway, it might not have been her. When you're new, you're always looking for familiar people and things. Whatever happened to her?

A: I have no idea. Maybe it could be her. Everybody's moving down here. Florida's like New York south. Let me know right away if you see HER again. I would like to say hello to her.

"So the mob is involved, huh?" Sir Red Herring said.

"Not all New Yorkers are in the mob, you know," Queens Quister objected.

"Oh, come on, I could practically smell the Aqua Velva through the monitor," Sir Red Herring laughed.

"The lady did say 'the family,'" Inspector Instinct pointed out.

"Well, maybe they have a big family. Look, I'm from Queens and believe me, not every New Yorker has connections," Queens Quister insisted.

"But some do, right?" Herring asked.

"Ok, yeah, I give up. There are some people who are involved," Queens Quister sighed.

"So, maybe she stole money from the mob and was on the run. This is a perfect place to hide. It's like AARP camouflage, hiding in plain sight," Herring laughed.

"Hmm, stolen money is not a bad idea. Daring Detective reported someone thought Willow was wealthy. That could make sense as a cover if she has ill-gotten gains," Instinct pondered.

"Could she have a cash stash somewhere?" Herring asked.

"I know the woman in the video. I'll go talk to her. Maybe she'll slip. We're both New Yorkers—we speak the same language," Quister said.

"Good, it's a language no one else understands anyway," Herring quipped.

"At least we're real people, not you're snooty upper-crust Richie Riches," Quister snidely responded.

"Quite, old girl," Herring said sarcastically. I can speak to Mayhem and Cluemaster to get access to her condo. Maybe there's a hidden safe or another place to hide money," Herring offered.

Queens Quister

Our restaurant was pretty nice—not a high-class joint but not a diner, either. It was decorated fancy, with a lot of glass and metal accents, high ceilings and tall curtains, but felt warm and comfortable. It was a popular hangout for residents. Some people ate there occasionally and some frequently, but the bar was the biggest attraction. It was a big circle that took up the center of the room and was decorated with an upscale ledge stone detail and leather stools with big backs. I hated barstools without a back— you have to be too stiff and you can't relax.

The bar had plenty of seating, as many people sat there and talked, watched ballgames, or just ate. They even have bar trivia a few nights a month, which draws a crowd. It's really the heart of the community—the evening gathering place.

Some people ate at the bar solo. It was easier to blend in when you were one of many at a bar. I remembered seeing the woman from the video at the bar right after canasta, so I made sure I was at there with a glass of Chianti when the game let out.

I needed to get her to talk to me, so I stopped her when she walked by me.

"Hey, honey, you look familiar. I think I know you from the old neighborhood, don't I?" I moved my bag so she could sit down.

"Do I? Sometimes I think everyone looks familiar here," she said and sat down.

"I know what you mean. I'm always looking for other refugees from the boroughs. Join me for a glass of Chianti?" I asked.

"Well, I guess maybe one. I know it's a 'fox paw' to drink it without food, but since you are too, I will. They have a wonderful selection here."

"Yes. Did you live in Sunnyside?" I asked.

"Oh, no, I'm originally from the Bronx, Morris Park Avenue, but now we live in Queens on 141st Street," she said.

"I'm from Queens too—155th street. I must have seen you in the butcher shop, Diva's nail salon or Gold's Deli?" I smiled.

"Yeah, how about that? Small world, ain't it?" she laughed.

"I don't think one day goes by that I don't see somebody I knew back in the old days. Last week I saw someone I went to P.S. 83 with. I hadn't seen her in fifty years. Isn't that a kick?"

I probed a little more. I wanted to see if she'd mention Willow or the family, but didn't want to go too quickly and scare her off.

"I never know who I'll see next." I expected a response but got nothing but a smile and a nod. I need a different tack.

"You said you still live in Queens, not Florida?" I asked.

"We come and go when my husband can get away," she said. "I don't know if I could ever leave New York. The weather is much better, but Florida's just not the same. Plus, I don't think my husband could ever retire," she said.

"I know about stubborn men. It took me years to convince mine to retire from the Garment District. He sold men's suits. He had four closets of them back in our apartment. He loved the people. I finally convinced him that in an active-adult community, you can talk to people all day and you don't have to sell them anything. Bet he's over at the billiards room talking to someone right now," I said.

"I'd like to come down here more, but my husband can't just retire. He's a big part of his organization," she said, happily sipping her wine.

That was enough for me. He can't retire from the organization. He's connected. But what about Willow? I needed to nudge her more.

"I know what you mean. My husband played ping pong the other day with a tailor who used to work at his shop. What are the odds? Maybe that old saying is right and people always travel in the same circles in life, because their souls seek each other out," I said.

Her glass was nearly empty. This was my last chance; I needed some information about Willow.

"You know, you may be right about that. Just the other day, I thought I saw this lady who used to work with my husband's boss. Maybe you've seen her. She's short with dark hair and she always wears red," she said.

"I have seen someone around who wears red shoes with flowers. Is that her?" I asked.

"I think so. I hope I see her again. My husband wants to see her too," she smiled and said goodbye.

She identified Willow. Bingo.

Sir Red Herring

Master Mayhem and I visited Willow's condo that night. It was the weekly dance party, so I thought most people would be at the community recreation center. It was very popular. Many residents enjoyed dancing in a group like they were teens again.

Armed with gloves and flashlights, we looked all around for a safe, strong box or hidden compartment where large sums of money could be concealed. We looked in every cabinet, behind every picture and in closets. We looked in all the drawers for a false front, back or bottom. Nothing.

The whole home was tiled and there was concrete between all the floors, so there was very little chance of a secret floor or ceiling compartments. Living in old New England estates all my life gave me a unique expertise in where to see what was meant to be unseen. These cloaked areas were as common in large estates as the butler's bell. I found it common for rich people are always hiding things from each other or the authorities.

Mayhem even brought a stud finder from his workshop to see if we could find a concealed niche behind the walls, but it was a big zero.

"We've exhausted every place I can think of. I'm starting to believe we let our imagination get the best of us. Maybe Willow had nothing to hide?" I said.

We both stood and looked around the room for inspiration.

"I know. My grandmother used to hide her money in pots in the stove. You know how Depression people didn't trust banks. She said it was like a safe because if there was a fire, the pots and oven wouldn't burn. But I never knew if she took the money out of the oven when she made dinner. I'll look there," Mayhem said.

"Good thinking. And I remember an old aunt who used to hide her pocket money under her mattress so my uncle wouldn't find it. I'll look there," I said.

While Mayhem was in the kitchen, I went to the bedroom and looked under the mattress. Nothing there either. I sat on the bed looking into the bathroom and saw it staring right at me. The toilet. I saw a movie once where a criminal stashed their money in the toilet tank. I lifted the lid and there it was—a waterproof bag hanging on the back of the toilet tank. And inside, there were four stacks of fifty-dollar bills. It looked like the stacks were each about an inch thick. A quick internet search on my phone showed there were two hundred and fifty bills in a one inch stack. If they were all fifties, that would be fifty thousand dollars.

"Pay dirt—these pots are full of twenties," Mayhem shouted from the kitchen.

I ran into the room and explained what I found in the bathroom and we counted and tallied the stash. There was one hundred thousand dollars. I thought most people would agree that's definitely more than walking around money.

We left the money right where we found it. Breaking and entering was one thing, but I drew the line at stealing. But the big question was, where did Willow get this kind of money and why was she hiding it?

Inspector Instinct

The team came through. Cash found, and we confirmed Willow's identity with the mob.

Maybe she was on the run. That would explain the hidden cash, the mob connections and the new credit and bank accounts. But while a hundred grand is a lot of money, it's really not enough to make an enemy of the mob and spend your life running. Then again, she could have spent some of it already.

My wife has a Realtor license and could look up the condo sale to see if there was a mortgage. And maybe someone could search her car title to see if it has a lien.

I hope to hear from my contacts in the Caymans soon. If she had accounts there, that could explain a lot.

Smoking Gun said he would look into her background. I need to see what he's comes up with.

Chapter 7

A Fine Mess:

Magnolia Mastermind

This was a fine mess we have to unravel, like old bunches of yarn tangled together in your crocheting bag. And Madame must have been pleased with my detective work, as she gave me two more videos from the secret camera footage to figure out. I'm so glad to have more clues to track down. I just loved the chase.

But I wanted to clear up that business with Iris first. It was bothering me, so I asked Sparks if we had any cameras in the creek area that could substantiate Iris's claim that Willow was alive when she left her.

He said there were no cameras there, but he was a crafty guy, that Sparks. He looked in the creek area and found a security camera, and then somehow got the footage for the day Iris and Willow were at the bridge.

I didn't know how he got it. Sometimes it was best not to ask these things. I was just glad he got it.

Sparks said the footage had no sound and was very grainy. And as the camera pivoted back and forth to get the whole area, the camera angle might not show whether Willow was there after Iris left. It was a long shot. He said he would look through it and join the team later.

In the meantime, Delta, Newshound and I watched the new videos Madame provided. Both videos were taken in the card room with neighbors talking about Willow. Madame named them *Mahjong Missing Persons* and *Porsche Puzzler*. Aren't those names just darling?

A: Where's everybody at? We were supposed to play mahjong today.

B: I don't know about the others, but there's a lot of talk about Willow. People say she's missing. I don't know about that, but I'm glad she's not here. She cheats.

A: No, she doesn't. She's just really competitive.

B: I've played with her before. She cheats. I've seen her draw extra tiles and palm them in her hand. She wins way too much and is always too quick to dump her rack so no one can see.

A: If Willow is missing, maybe the others are too. Maybe something's going on. I read a book where people were kidnapped for their Social Security checks and AARP benefits.

B: You read too many books. No one's taking seniors so they can get cheap movie tickets.

A: You never know. Human trafficking is a thing. Young women, children and even young men are taken for any number of horrible reasons. Maybe seniors are next.

B: Ooooo, maybe there's alien abductor stealing seniors for bridge tournaments on Mars.

A: Very funny, really, I heard about some missing foursomes at golf the other day. They never showed up for their tee times. You never know.

B. Hold that thought. Here's a text from one of our missing players. She lost track of time.

A: Willow?

B: No.

A: What about the others?

B: Hold on, I'm asking if they were abducted by aliens. She laughed. She doesn't know about Willow, but our fourth had to go up north for a family emergency. See, no need for a Florida Silver Alert Notice. Everyone accounted for.

A: Except Willow.

"Well, that's useless," Newshound said. "We need facts, not stupid conspiracy theories about alien abduction. This is Peacock Perch, not Area 51."

"I do love a good book about intrigue, and there are a lot of accounts of people getting abducted and even more mystery shrouded with Area 51 and Roswell," Delta countered.

"Aliens aren't real." Newshound said. "But I've read a lot about human trafficking in the news recently. That is a possible assumption, but I don't know what criminal traffickers would want with senior citizens."

"Social Security checks and AARP discounts!" Delta snapped.

"I can't say I know diddly about aliens, but I did know a few men when I was a young girl in Georgia who disappeared and then reappeared with no explanation, but we all just figured they were on a bender or having their needs satisfied elsewhere," I added. "Anyhow, let's look at the next video. Remember, this was also taken in the card room on a different day with a Bridge foursome."

A: Did anyone hear about Willow Wisteria? She's missing!

B: Oh, she probably went off with the Porsche guy—her boyfriend.

C: I haven't seen him OR his fancy car in over a week. It's been at least that long since I've seen her.

D: Is he the one she brought to the dance?

A: No, that was a young guy; this is a rich guy. You know Willow, she parades different men around here all the time. I've seen them at the restaurant together.

D: How do you know he's rich?

B: He's rich. I heard he throws fifty-dollar bills at the servers here. Plus, I've seen that Porsche 911 Turbo S in her parking space. I looked it up online and saw a similar one for $273,000. Now I'm no expert, but that screams rich to me!

D: Well, that's it; she's probably on some nice vacation with her rich boyfriend.

A: I don't think so; she always brags about her boyfriends buying her things. If she was going on a fancy vacation, everyone in Peacock Perch would know about it.

C: You're right. That is strange.

"Sounds to me like this Willow is a person of low degree," Magnolia said.

"I don't know what that means, but how are we going to find out who these men are?" Newshound asked.

"Maybe the security cameras at the entrance can get a license plate on the Porsche," I said. "We can ask Sparks, he should be here any minute with the security footage at the creek."

"Why did they have a security camera there?" Delta asked.

"I heard my name. I have something to show you." Sparks entered and put his laptop on the table.

"To answer your question, Delta, the security people told me they were worried people were going around the bridge barriers to see the baby alligators and could get hurt, so they placed a camera out there to warn people if they went there." Sparks explained.

"Is anyone getting uncomfortable with all these cameras out there watching our every move?" Delta asked nervously.

"I don't know. It helps us, but you need to watch yourself," Sparks said.

"Big Brother's watching," Newshound laughed.

"Ok, y'all, we have a job to do. Let's see what Sparks found," I said.

"Right, first, let's look at the footage with Iris. There's Iris and Willow at the bridge. Notice the broken railing. Willow goes on the bridge and takes the picture of Iris and the baby alligators. Then Iris goes up there, gets the phone from her and leaves with Willow still on the bridge."

"Well, I guess that's it. Iris is in the clear," I said.

"Wait—do you see that?" Newshound asked. "Willow is typing on her phone, but is that another person coming toward her? A man?"

"Yes, that looks like a man to me," Delta said.

"Exactly, someone else was out there, but then the camera moved away from the bridge and when it returned around, we see the railing is now completely missing, but nothing else," Sparks said.

"So that's it. Someone else came and pushed her off the bridge," Delta said.

"Or Iris came back and did it. You couldn't really see who was coming toward Willow in the picture. It could be Iris," Newshound said.

"I don't think so. No one knew these cameras were out there. Why would she come back?" Sparks said.

"Maybe the man on the bridge was one of her boyfriends!" Delta said and excitedly opened her folder. "I was looking through the dossier about the younger boyfriend and there were some Nosy Neighbor posts in about him."

I'm getting sick of some people and their rated "R" activity around here. I didn't move here for Peyton Place.

Are you talking about the skimpy bathing suits? I'm sorry, but I don't think small bikinis, thongs and Speedos are appropriate for our type of community.

Prudes!! Don't look if you don't like it. Some of us may like some eye candy once in a while. Although, some people should look in the mirror before going to the pool.

Relax. Live and let live if you ask me.

FREE WILLY! lol.

Really? No, I'm talking about public displays of affection by the pool and at the dances. Some people need to get a room.

CALM DOWN! We're all just here to have fun.

I agree. I've seen a little too much of a certain "lady" and a greasy young man walking around here in his skin tight pants.

Speak for yourself. I don't mind seeing that young Greek god around here with his wavy hair and dreamy accent. If you don't want to see it, don't look or stay home.

"So this boyfriend has a Greek accent—that's one clue." Delta said. "I'm pretty friendly with the staff here. Let me see what I can find out about the other boyfriend, the rich Porsche guy, throwing big bills at them. And they might remember the accent, but then again everyone around here has different accents. It's like the United Nations."

"Sparks, before you came in, we saw a video about another boyfriend that drove a Porsche. Aren't there cameras at the front gate? Maybe they could get a license plate?" I asked.

"Sure, I help security at the guardhouse with electrical issues sometimes. I could ask them to check the tapes for the Porsche to look for a license plate," Sparks offered. "And I'll check the camera feeds to see if I can find someone meeting the young Greek guy's description," Sparks added.

"While I don't believe in aliens, I'd like to look into this trafficking angle and whether there are really multiple people missing. This may not be an instance of one missing person, but an epidemic," Newshound said.

"Good plans y'all," I said. "I am going to mosey on down to the card room and play a few hands of cards. Everybody gets real loose playing bridge. I can get any information from people in a card game. In a tournament, I could probably even get ATM numbers."

On my way to the card room, I was still on the fence about Iris. She told me everything very calmly and clearly, but I just couldn't get over that strange smile when she talked about Willow getting punished. It was almost sinister. I thought she was talking about the suspension letter, but I was really not sure. I guess we need to keep Iris on the suspect list for now.

Luckily, the card room wasn't too full. Fewer people made for better conversations. I joined a few people and put my little plan into motion. I took the incensed route, which always gets lips flapping.

"I'm happy for some normality after the public spectacles I've been seeing around here," I baited.

"What do you mean?" one man asked.

"Open your eyes. I know what she's talking about. I've seen making out on the dance floor and at the pool. They were just talking about it on Nosy Neighbors," one lady said.

"I do believe it was Willow with a young foreign man," I probed further.

"Yes. It's disgusting. I haven't seen them for a while, but she parades that man around and just rubs all our noses in it. His tight pants, slicked back hairy chest," another lady said.

"His chest hair is slicked back?" the man laughed.

"No, his hair is slicked back, and he has a hairy chest," she huffed.

"I don't know where in the world one meets these types of men," I prodded.

"I sure don't care to know," she said.

Dead end. I played my hand out and then excused myself to powder my nose. But in the bathroom, a woman told me the story of Willow and that young man.

"I heard you talking about Willow and that young Greek. He was a gigolo, she paid him. Her neighbor told me she saw Willow giving the kid a big wad of money on more than one occasion," she rattled.

She left me alone in the bathroom with a big fat puzzle in my lap. Would someone actually pay for "services" like that? Seemed like the more answers we discovered, more questions come up.

The next day, I ran into Delta and Sparks at the community center. They were both coming to find me, so we sat down at the outside coffee bar and I told them about the gigolo theory.

"That tracks with my information too," Delta said. "I talked to a couple of the servers in the dining room and they said the Porsche guy didn't throw big bills at them. Willow did. They said she always paid with fifty-dollar bills."

"There were a few Porsches on the front entrance camera feed for the last two months, but only one that came in and out on the same day and time every week. But it hadn't been here in for the last two weeks. The security guard did me a favor and asked a copy friend to run the plate. And the car was registered to Willow. It looks like Willow was loaded." Sparks said.

"And one more thing—a resident overheard my conversation with the servers and told me she thinks Willow was a prostitute. We talked about that possibility with the others before" Delta nodded her head enthusiastically.

"I don't believe it. I've seen Willow—no one's getting rich from that," Sparks laughed and tipped back in his chair.

"Now just a second, funny man," Delta scolded. "It is possible. There are a lot of lonely men here who may feel safe with someone here. But I don't know where the Greek guy and the Porsche guy come into this. It appears she was paying them."

"If she paid them, was she working for them or were they working for her? Maybe she was the pimp and they were all working… so to speak." Sparks asked.

"Oh my! My goodness. Pimps, prostitutes, gigolos? This still sounds unsavory to me. I need to report all this back to Madame. I will be in touch with our next assignment. Keep your eyes and ears open," I said, overwhelmed and left to find Madame.

I really didn't know what to make of all this. The whole affair was as repugnant as a prize pig in a prom dress and tiara waving from a county parade float. Yuck!

Chapter 8

Disappearances:

Delta Snoops

I knew everyone thought the alien idea was nonsense, but I just knew it could be possible. After all, I was the reigning Southwest Florida jigsaw puzzle champion. I knew how to fit together puzzles. I saw them in my head and the pieces just seemed to come together magically.

And Magnolia wasn't the only one who grew up with alien abduction suspicions. When I was a little girl growing up in southern Mississippi, there were several instances of people just disappearing. Working on the gulf rigs, many people were transient, so some thought it was normal.

One old man I knew saw circular impressions in his muddy field that he swore were spaceships about once a month. And a few days after he saw them, each time, there were rumblings about people disappearing. Some came back without any understanding of where they were, and others never returned.

He kept track of everything in a big scrapbook. He showed me the pictures and the timelines he drew up. He tried to ask some NASA fellas about it, but they shut him down right quick. He said they were scared by what he showed them and tried to take the pictures, but he got away. He knew he was onto something. I think he was too.

I saw these posts on the Nosy Neighbors app. I didn't show them to anyone yet. I need more evidence. No one believes me.

> *Did anyone see strange lights on the golf course last night?*

> *I saw it too. The party you're talking about was on the other side. I was walking my dog. This was on the 3rd green.*

> *Exactly! It was a strange glow.*

> *I think some young people in the next neighborhood were having a party with a DJ and some disco lights.*

I saw it too. It didn't look like disco lights to me. It was one beam of light.

OOOH. Maybe it's aliens. Look out. LOL

Stop being mean. If two people saw something, it must have been there.

It's not aliens! Stop spreading rumors.

If it is aliens, I hope they get you next.

Maybe it was a plane or something.

Or maybe it was a something...

Newshound

I could be barking up the wrong tree, but my infallible nose for news told me there's something here. I spent thirty years as a newspaper reporter and I got a certain sense anytime I smelled a news story coming on. I've been retired for years, but it just doesn't go away.

I knew the alien hypothesis was a stupid fairytale, but seniors go missing every year and many times it was foul play. Most live alone, so if their family doesn't keep up with them, or they have no family, it could be weeks before anyone reports their absence.

I looked into it and last year there was a story in town that ran for two months about an older woman who disappeared. She had dementia, so they thought she wandered off. After a big manhunt, she never turned up, but they later found a credit card in her name was being used long after she disappeared. Someone killed her, dumped her body and stole her identity to create credit card accounts in her name.

I also read about a young woman who was a caretaker for an older man. He died of natural causes, but she didn't report his death so she could live in the home rent-free, collect her paycheck and keep the monthly allowance she received for groceries. And if she needed to buy anything extra, she just called his estate attorney for money. It seemed normal. He had no children, so no one was paying attention. She was caught when a neighbor's dog accidentally dug up the old man's body. She buried him in a vacant lot near the house.

So while the AARP benefit idea was going up the wrong path, there was a reason to abduct seniors—money.

But finding out who's missing in a senior community is a tough thing to get a handle on. People come and go visiting friends and relatives and traveling around. The one great thing about retirement is you get to complete that bucket list, with new experiences and seeing everything you were too busy to notice before.

Plus, there are the seasonal owners who live here for a few months and live somewhere else the other time. And some people cloister in their homes for health or other reasons, so no one sees them.

But there was one person in the community who knew if people were going away for a while—the mail lady.

Our community didn't have individual mailboxes in front of each house, like in most neighborhoods. Instead, there were big kiosks where all the mailboxes in the neighborhood were located in one place.

The same mail lady delivered to our entire community for years, so she got to know everyone very well. And most would forward or stop their mail when they traveled, so she knew who got mail and who didn't. She told me once that as a reminder, she put a colored card in their mailbox if the mail was on hold, so she wouldn't accidentally put any mail in their box.

I've been chummy with the mail lady for a long time. I gave her gifts and saw her every day. We talked about our families, friends, interests and everything else. She always had the best gossip. Plus, she was cute, and I had a little crush on her.

"I see you're using yellow this month for our wayward neighbors. They almost match these flowers."

I smiled and gave her some jasmine flowers from my garden. I cultivate several varieties around my lanai. They're pretty and have a rich smell that fills the air with a palpable aroma you could almost taste. Poets often describe it as an animalistic, intoxicating or sensual aphrodisiac. I figured it could help me with the ladies.

She giggled and took a deep sniff to inhale the sweet fragrance.

"I just have to see this beautiful garden you keep telling me about," she smiled and said in her sugary Southern twang. "I'm using yellow in this neighborhood, but I have orange, green and pink in some others. This month I have to use all my cards because a lot of people are away."

"Oh, I always wondered about that," I prodded. "What if people don't stop their mail and don't pick up it up for a long time? These boxes are so small, they don't fit a lot."

"That happens all the time. Some people don't pick up their mail for a week and I have to stuff everything in the box. I have one older lady who doesn't walk well, and she only comes once a week or so. If it gets too full, I take the mail to her home," she said.

"You're so sweet. I could imagine some people would take advantage of your good nature. Anyone who hasn't picked up their mail in a long time? I would be happy to take the mail to them for you."

"Oh, you are just the kindest man I ever laid eyes on. I'm not supposed to, but honestly, that would be a huge help. I have to do this whole neighborhood by myself and sometimes there's not enough time to be kind.

"There actually are a couple new ones recently that I don't know about; one in the Parrot condos, one in the Pelican townhomes, and one in the Pheasant villas. I don't know any of them and none of them picked the mail up in weeks. I knocked on the doors a few times a week ago and no one answered. I keep them in bags in my car, waiting for them to get their mail so I can load more." She smiled coyly and handed me the three bags.

I quickly glanced at the names, but none of them was Willow.

"I'm going to play cards with a couple of friends in a little while. As I've been deputized as a temporary mail carrier, maybe I'll pick up their mail for them too."

I gave her Willow's unit number, 230, along with a couple others in the Parrot condos to throw her off.

"Here's the mail for these two, but 230 doesn't have any mail in it," she said.

"Oh, she must have picked it up already?" I said.

I chitchatted with her a little while more and left to check out the three addresses she gave me. They could also be missing persons.

As I drove my golf cart to the homes, I was puzzled about Willow's mail. If she'd been gone for a few weeks, why was there no mail? Didn't she get mail? Did someone pick it up?

I went to the Pheasant villa first. There were no shutters on the windows. It was common when people left town for an extended period to put their shutters up, but some people had hurricane-proof windows and no need for shutters. I rang the bell and knocked on the door several times. Nothing.

Since many Floridians lived outdoors on their lanais, I walked around to the back. No one was there, so I tried the lanai door. It was unlocked, so I carefully ventured in and was promptly met by a barking dog with snarling teeth. I dropped the bag and ran out as fast as I could. I figured if the dog was out, there must be someone inside.

The second was in the Pelican townhomes. Again, I rang the bell and knocked on the door. Nothing. Some people could be gone and forgot to stop the mail and some could just be out for the day. I looked through the windows to see if I could see anyone, when someone came up behind me.

"What are you doing? Who are you?" she asked.

"Oh, hi. I was delivering their mail. The box is full." I was startled by her abrupt and surprisingly stealthy approach.

"I'll take it. I was supposed to pick that up for her and I forgot. I'm her neighbor," she said.

"I don't know. I'm only supposed to give it to the addressee," I hesitated.

"Look, I have her garage door code. She's up North visiting family." She opened the garage door, so I gave her the mail.

With two down and no leads, I figured I may be barking up the wrong tree after all. But then I arrived at the Parrot condos. I knocked on the door and rang the bell. Nothing. I glanced around for anyone who might sneak up on me and then looked in the window, when I saw a foot on the floor peeking through the open doorway inside the condo.

I called 911 and tried to find a hidden key under a mat or atop a doorway to open the front door. Then I saw a little frog pot next to the door and reached into its open mouth. There was a key!

I opened the door to find a man lying on the floor unconscious. He had a weak heartbeat and was still breathing, but he wouldn't come to. His face was covered in sweat and his shirt collar was damp. Then I noticed an insulin meter on his belt.

I had a friend who was diabetic, and if his insulin was very low, he would sweat profusely on his forehead unless he had a jolt of glucose.

By then, the ambulance arrived. I told them I thought he was in diabetic shock. They checked his readings and gave him some kind of IV. After about fifteen minutes, he slowly opened his eyes, disoriented.

"Lucky you were here. You saved his life." The paramedics patted me on the back as they took him to the hospital.

They told me his insulin meter was old and malfunctioned. He said he was out cold for nearly a day. If I hadn't found him, who knows?

A good deed was done, but it looked like my hypothesis had run its course. Maybe there were missing seniors, but the only one in Peacock Perch that I still needed to look for was Willow Wisteria.

Chapter 9

The Accident:

Smoking Gun

I joined this group because I was getting a little itchy. I'm not typically a "joiner." I played golf, but mostly so I can bet on the holes. I liked to gamble. It was such a sucker's bet.

And I liked to watch people—a former occupational habit. It was like a new play unfolding every day right before my eyes. I watched, I listened and I learned.

People were peculiar. That's why I liked to work alone. I knew stuff, so they let me do my thing. No one got in my way.

I got a chuckle at how the amateurs in the group were baffled by the absence of a body. In my experience, getting rid of a body is the easy part.

But I played along with the "missing" theory. So, I checked this broad out. She was clean. No record, not even a parking ticket. Too clean.

Her background check showed she was born in Boston and that was it—just a birth certificate. It didn't indicate any diplomas, marriage certificates or any births, so no kids. Nothing was registered in her name until two years ago, in Florida—just the condo and two cars, an Audi and a Porsche.

No marriage or kids, that was possible, but in my former line of work, I saw a lot of records and an equal number of fakes. I could usually smell the fakes. This one was good, I'll give it that. It could be real, but I didn't think so. There was too much of a gap. People's lives were not that simple. I wanted to dig some more.

This whole camera footage drivel seemed like a waste of time to me, so I didn't want to be involved in any of that. I never dealt in hearsay; I only trusted facts—just the facts.

I didn't use social media myself. I liked to keep my life private, close to the vest. But I knew plenty of crooks who loved it. Social media gave a personal profile of every sucker out there. All they needed to do was read. And if a crook wanted to find out more, they posted phony memes, polls and questions and people commented and volunteered every piece of information about themselves.

Some people post everything in their lives. Vacations. Memories of their first dates. First car or where they met their spouse. Birthday and anniversary greetings for everyone. Kids, parents, and pet names. Right down to what they had for dinner and where.

People even posted when they're not home and gave all the information a criminal needed for passwords. Totally a sucker's bet.

It was a treasure chest of information right there for the taking. So I scanned the social media posts and something caught my eye. A bunch of hens were yapping about some near accident in the community.

Does anyone know why an ambulance was in the compound today?

I heard it was a hit-and-run?

Oh, no! Who was hit? Are they OK?

I heard it was someone walking in the crosswalk.

No. I think it was a bicycle.

Someone posted it was a golf cart.

I'm not surprised. All of the speeding and running stop signs has got to stop!

Was it a resident?

The driver or the walker?

Either! Both!

People are in too much of a hurry. Relax – we're retired. We have plenty of time.

Speak for yourself.

That driver ought to be kicked out of Peacock Perch.

It could have been a delivery person or a contractor. They are always speeding on our streets and never get caught.

We need more police patrols.

We DO NOT need police patrols!

Get a grip! Accidents happen. And sometimes the bikers and joggers don't pay attention.

The kid who works in the golf shop told me that the golfer who heard the crash was really upset. He said he heard a woman screaming and then a car drove off.

Wow, my neighbor said she was nearly hit by a black limo racing out of the subdivision around the same time.

It wasn't an ambulance. I heard it was a coroner's van.

Oh my god – the woman was killed?

Sounded like this was another possibility, but it was hard to sift through all the jumble.

If it was the broad, Willow, was she killed or not? That should be easy to find out. I could make a few calls and check police records.

The limo sighting is interesting. People used to hire limos all the time to go to and from the airports, but now they have Uber and Lyft, so I haven't seen one in a while. And no one in the perch owns a limo. People here were well off, but not that well off. There were a lot of Cadillacs, BMWs, Lexuses, maybe a Jag here and there, but no one had a limo and a driver.

I needed to see if someone could get the guard gate footage for that time. Maybe we could get a license plate and look it up. Plus, I wanted to talk to that golfer and see what he knew. Maybe he saw something a little more concrete.

The social media posts offered some clues, but I didn't know what was reliable and what was gossip. It's an old tale, even if people were in the same place at the same time, everyone saw and heard something different. I've said it before—people were peculiar.

Chapter 10

The 19th Hole:

Smoking Gun

The kid at the pro shop said the golfer who heard the hit-and-run was always at the "19th Hole," the golf club bar around 3pm. It was an inside joke that golfers always refer to the club bar as the 19th hole, because it was the last place they play. It was accurate, if nothing else.

The pro shop kid didn't know anything, just what the golfer told him. Good to know one thing about social media was accurate. After I fleeced my foursome—I meant after my golf game—I went to the bar and see what I could find out.

The bar of a golf club was a ritual. After nine or eighteen holes, the golfers came back and toast their conquests on the course, made jokes and had fun with each other. Both men and women golfers obeyed this tradition, but usually in separate places. In this bar, there were two distinct sides. It wasn't a written rule or anything, but it seemed purposeful.

The men's side was dark, with a lot of wood paneling and green walls; it was closest to the small bar. There were tables, so most people sat there and relaxed in the shell-shaped leather club chairs.

The women's side was decorated with linen-covered tables arrayed along the windows. It was bright and sunny, with the tall drapes framing each window. The women's side was still considered the bar, but was closer to the restaurant and the women ordered their drinks from a server instead of shouting their orders to the nearby bartender. Different strokes and all.

I found a few guys sitting at a table by the bar. One of the men met the description the pro shop kid gave me. He was looking at his phone, while the others were regaling each other with their feats on the links.

"Are you reading Mugbook? I was looking for an update on that hit-and-run accident in the community," I asked, approaching him.

"No, I just look at the pictures of my grandkids." He abruptly put his phone down, like it embarrassed him to be looking at social media.

"Hey, you're the big winner. I hear you cleaned up out there today," another golfer said to me.

"Gentlemen, you know that no one can monetarily benefit from playing golf at this club," I said sarcastically.

We all simultaneously laughed, and they asked me to sit down. Of course, there was betting on each hole, the game, the shot, everything. I got more action on the links than I ever did at the track. I once heard of four men racing their golf carts to each hole and betting on the winner. Good thing they weren't racing for pinks. What anyone would do with more than one golf cart? Like I said, I loved a sucker's bet. I won, suckers lost.

But betting was against club policy. So, a gentleman's agreement was supposed to keep it mum. The funny thing was everyone talked about it freely. These guys weren't big on keeping secrets.

"I was hoping Mugbook had some new information on that hit-and-run a couple weeks ago. My wife and I go bike riding every day, but she won't go since she heard someone was hit. I would think they would have concrete information by now," I said.

"I don't read it myself, but my wife does. She keeps blabbing about that missing woman, Willow Wisteria? No one has seen her for a month?" one golfer said.

"I heard that too. I wondered if she was the one involved in the hit-and-run. They said it was a woman." I poked a little more to get something started.

"I also understood a golfer witnessed the whole thing and reported it," another man said.

"Well, that's not technically accurate. I wasn't an eyewitness—I just overheard it. I was setting up a great putt and right in my backswing out of nowhere I heard a tire screech, like a car stopping quickly, and then a woman screaming. Then the car revved up and drove away quickly. That was it. I forgot my phone, so I drove right back to the club and told the pro shop kid to report it. I don't know what happened after that."

So much for the pro kid and the posts being right about anything; you either couldn't trust social media or you couldn't trust men talking in a golf bar. Or both!

"I don't know about the hit-and-run, but I know I saw Willow recently. I passed her putting on my way to the clubhouse late one afternoon. I remember I saw her red golf cart with all the flowers on it," one man said.

"Do you remember when that was? A lot of people are talking about her missing," I asked.

"I think it was last week. It's hard to remember," the man said.

"People talk about her all the time. She's an odd bird," another man said.

"She's a bit of a nuisance at the club. She plays by herself after hours at dusk to avoid paying greens fees," another said.

"No, she plays alone because no one will play with her, since the club sanctioned her for cheating," one man corrected.

"She's always making trouble. My wife says no one in the pottery class likes her because she hogs the kiln," another said.

"Yeah, that's the reason she's missing. Someone killed her for ruining a pot," one man laughed and the others followed.

"I know, maybe she's not putting, but doing a satanic ritual and howling at the moon," one laughed.

"My wife said she was a bitch—not a witch," he laughed.

"Hey, maybe she got struck by lightning and eaten by coyotes," another joked.

"Didn't the pro say several foursomes didn't show up today? Maybe she's an alien kidnapping golfers and taking them to the mother ship," one of them chuckled.

"Better send out one of those Silver Alerts," a man quipped. "Culprit was last seen on a golf course in a silver spaceship, license plate Andromeda 51."

A few drinks in, everyone was laughing and joking so much, I figured the window for useful information had passed. I started to make my escape to avoid another hour and a few drinks of more unhelpful jocularity, when the club bartender stopped me.

"Were you guys talking about a red golf cart with flowers on it?" he asked. "That golf cart was in the parking lot for about a week. They tried to contact the owner but couldn't, so they put it in the club garage a week ago. But then it disappeared. I assumed the owner came to get it."

So, is this dame missing or not? The bartender's timeline of two weeks is consistent with all the other evidence, so it's possible the golfer who saw her on the course was just mixing up his weeks. It happens. Sometimes I felt like there's a beginning of the month and an end of the month and nothing in between. But then who came to pick up the golf cart?

This case got stranger by the minute. I made some calls to my police sources on the hit-and-run. There was no police report and no call to paramedics. So there was no ambulance, no coroner, no police—nothing.

Of course, you couldn't go by the gossip, but someone said they saw an ambulance, and another said they saw a coroner's van. They wouldn't both be wrong—right? Or maybe they were? You needed to filter through the garbage in social media to find the truth, if there's any. Reading these posts was like a puzzle in itself. A social media account was like a license to tell tall tales.

I met up with Sparks in the lounge. He had a line on the security camera footage at the community entrance gate and called to let me know he had some information.

"Here's the license plate for the black car spotted on the day of the hit-and-run," Sparks said and showed me a picture of the license plate. "It wasn't a limo, just an old black Caddy. And the license plate is not on file with security, so it was an outside car. But the guard gate had no record of anyone coming in with that car. We got the plate from the camera at the outgoing gate."

I looked at the picture file. It was a New York plate. Now, that's interesting. I had an old neighborhood friend in

New York who can run this plate down. Maybe that could put some pieces of this puzzle together.

Chapter 11

Follow the Money:

Inspector Instinct

The community library was one of my favorite places. I liked the big comfy chairs with high backs for privacy. I read the paper and books, drank coffee and watched people. The library was next to the coffee lounge and the de facto main traffic pattern to the exercise facility. I think everyone in the community came in and out of here on a daily basis.

Sitting in my favorite chair, I was trying to piece things together in my mind. There were too many loose ends in this case. I couldn't help thinking about the money. In a mystery, detectives always say, "follow the money."

I talked to my banking friends in the Caymans, but it was a dead end. They didn't have any record of anyone with Willow's name or address in their system. They were pretty strict with anonymity protocols, but they definitely require identification to open accounts.

My wife looked into her condo deed and verified there was no recorded mortgage. Smoking Gun's connections found the same thing about her Audi and the Porsche; no liens were filed. So, it was possible that she paid cash for her condo and the cars. That could account for half of a million dollars right there.

Although that was not unusual in Florida; people often used the proceeds of their home sale up North to buy with cash.

Her credit card bills ran about six thousand per month and were paid off. And her five bank accounts all added up to only about fifteen thousand dollars total, so how did she pay off six thousand in credit card bills each month with just social security?

I never trusted anyone who had several bank accounts. It might be perfectly innocent, but keeping small amounts in each account could be one way to fly under the banking radar, not to trigger any alerts for deposits in terms of size or frequency. That was a trick I saw many times in my former life to launder cash from illegal pursuits.

And then there was the one hundred-thousand-dollar cash stash. That money had to come from something under the table. Maybe not illegal, but she obviously didn't want a paper trail.

Finally, there was the source who said she inherited a fortune. Without knowing where or when, it's very difficult to trace. That could account for how she spends more than she gets, but the only reason to keep it off the books is to evade taxes or suspicion. Inheritance had to go through probate courts, so it would be difficult to conceal that. Many people avoided taxes with cash businesses, but that was a lot of money to keep in toilets and pots.

What were you up to, Willow? No one stashed that much money in their home unless they have something to hide.

Delta Snoops was not the only jigsaw puzzle aficionado in the group. This case was like when some pieces fit together well, but there are some missing pieces that keep the whole thing from coming together… and they're under the couch where you can't find them.

Just then, Red Herring sat down and woke me out of my puzzle stupor. He said he had some news.

"I have a confession to make," he said with his head down. He pulled two bottles from his pocket.

I recognized the bottles as the ones we found in Willow's condo in the boxes of lotions and essential oils.

"What are you doing with those?" I asked.

"That's my crime. Mayhem pocketed some of the bottles the last time he was in the condo for his wife. He gave me a couple for my wife too, but when she used them, it made her break out in a rash. She has very sensitive skin."

He showed me pictures of her arms with red bumps all over them.

"So I gave the bottles to Cluist to analyze. He said they're not lotions and essential oils—the main ingredient is cannabis and THC. They're cannabidiol (CBD) and liquid marijuana," Herring explained.

"Ok, but so what? This is a retirement—I mean active-adult community. CBD is like sunscreen here. It's not illegal," I replied.

"I have no personal knowledge of this, of course. I toked a few here and there back in the day, but this is a whole new industry. According to my research, CBD made from hemp is not illegal, but when made from cannabis/THC (tetrahydrocannabinol) it is illegal here in Florida," he added.

"Liquid weed? What will they think of next? I said. "But still, medical marijuana is legal in the state and pretty easy for seniors to get, from what I hear. There are more medical marijuana cards in this community than golf carts."

"Yes, but from what I understand, liquid weed is not as prevalent in the dispensaries, especially in this high concentration. People use the liquid in vape pens and in drinks—THC cocktails they call them. Remember how lethal Everclear was? High doses of this liquid marijuana could be even deadlier," he said.

"Then she had enough for a whole army... or a whole community," I said.

Herring said he was late for a ping pong match and had to leave. After filling up another cup of coffee, I sat down in my deep-cushioned chair and thought some more.

Dealing could explain some of the cash stockpiles she had, and disguising the liquid marijuana in essential oils and lotions was a very clever. And using the massage business as a front, even down to the Happy Endings supplier in New York, was brilliant. We were obviously not dealing with an amateur here.

It was one more piece to the puzzle, but I didn't think it was the missing piece. Even if the theory were true, how did it explain her disappearance?

And the amount of money still bothered me. Could she make that much money selling little bottles of marijuana to her neighbors? If we counted the condo, cars and cash, we're talking close to a million dollars. It may be just another unrelated rabbit hole. But money often led to the crime.

I finished my last cup and was heading to take a walk to clear my head when I ran into Minx coming from the tennis courts.

"Glad I ran into you. I just had an interesting discussion with a neighbor of Willow's between tennis matches. We were talking about how bad cell phone service is in the condos and she said she overheard a man outside on Willow's balcony a couple of weeks ago talking on the phone. She only heard one side of the conversation, of course, but she said she heard the man say, 'I took it away from her' and 'I know what to do about her now,'" she said.

"Why is she just reporting this?" I asked.

"She's been out of town for a month. Her daughter just had twins and she's been helping her care for them, so she didn't hear about Willow until today. The people at the tennis courts were buzzing about Willow. It's all anyone can talk about," Minx said.

Sometimes it seemed like I was putting together several puzzles with similar pictures and then it all fell on the floor. Maybe her drug partners were trying to cut her out? Nothing fit and there were more pieces everywhere.

Chapter 12

The Clues:

Smoking Gun

When you had a particular set of skills… and certain rare contacts… people gave you difficult tasks to perform.

The phone Magnolia and Delta found near the creek came into my possession. Now, I hardly knew a cellphone from a transistor radio, but I knew people who knew things. Frankly, I hated these smartphones. They made me feel dumb, overcomplicating things with this app and that. It was too much to learn. I liked to keep things simple.

But I found a smart phone was a necessary evil to have so many helpful tools at my fingertips. And in my business, a phone, a camera, a video camera and email were very useful. Plus, I loved having any information I wanted, only a voice command away.

So I made a few calls and got some people to work on the waterlogged phone. It was pretty messed up. The screen was cracked and they drained muddy water from it. They brought it back to life, barely, and cracked the pass code—1-2-3-4. Really? So inventive.

Most of the phone was damaged beyond repair. The only thing they could get was the last screen, which seemed to be frozen, maybe when the phone was dropped. It was a series of text messages.

Not exactly a smoking gun, but not innocent either. It really could be anything. Someone was threatening Willow with something. Could have been a breakup, a business deal gone awry, or maybe someone was going to report her.

But in my experience, a murderer does not announce his or her intentions to the victim in advance. So while I didn't treat this as a confession, it could have been a clue as to who could be a suspect. Unfortunately, the phone number of the person couldn't be recovered. The only thing we got was the contact name…"Him."

So we can assume it's a man, but nothing else. What a strange way to refer to someone in a phone. If I were a headshrinker, I would say that's a sarcastic tone. It doesn't sound like a love interest, but definitely someone you want to keep secret; otherwise, why not put at least their first name or a nickname?

Our current suspect list had several men. I'm not saying this eliminated the women on the list, but this clue directly pointed to a man.

The New York license plate was a different story. I called an associate in New York and they found the owner of the car is a company in New York… the Happy Endings Massage Company.

By no coincidence, that was the name on all the boxes delivered to Willow's condo. So, I called a few other associates and learned the Happy Endings Massage Company was reportedly related to a certain family in the New York mob who were well known for their enterprising business connections in the procurement and delivery industries—smuggling.

If that family was mixed up in this, it could get very sticky. They were not a very friendly organization.

I went over to the recreation center to find Inspector Instinct. He's always in the library drinking coffee. Either he loves the coffee there, he doesn't like his home or he was getting away from his wife. Who knows? Maybe he just liked to sit there and people-watch. That could be an illuminating hobby.

I joined him for a cup and told him about the phone and the New York connection. He nearly spilled his coffee.

"This connects with the information I just received. The lotions and oils we found contained cannabis CBD and THC, liquid marijuana. Willow was dealing here in the perch and getting the stuff from that company in New York," Instinct said.

"Many organizations deal in this type of trade. Easy to manufacture and move. Legal or illegal, it's a growing business. And the text messages on her phone we recovered indicated someone was ready to inform on her," I said and showed him the phone screen.

"It fits a lot of pieces in the puzzle. Maybe the boyfriends were her dealers inside or outside the community. They would need to make frequent trips and she would need to pay them. And it is a cash business. But did one of them make those threats against her? Maybe they wanted to edge her out of the business?" Instinct said.

I left Instinct and walked back to my car. I wasn't sure the gigolos were on the right path. I didn't know what it was. For me, it just didn't connect. She had the New York source, and living here in this community, it would be easy for her to sell this at every activity and event. Young men would stand out in this community. They could be dealing outside, that's true, but they wouldn't have access without her. No, it doesn't fit.

The most promising theory was the New York connection. Why would they send a car all the way down here to take care of business? How was she associated with them? Did she double cross them? Was she abducted? Or if the car did hit her, where was the body?

In Florida, it would be even easy to dispose of a body. There are ponds everywhere and the gators will make quick work of that. You wouldn't even need concrete.

I needed to make some calls and find out more about this family and see if I could link anything back to Willow.

Chapter 13

The Puzzle:

Madame Sleuth

I called the sleuths together for a meeting to discuss and decipher the many clues we gathered. This case took so many unexpected twists, curves and some u-turns, it was a bit confusing. So, I created this intricate web to illustrate the suspects. The blue strings led to possible motives and the red strings guided to the means of murder. Quite impressive, I thought. Now, with the proper tools, we could get to brass tacks and solve this case.

"I called this meeting so we can put our heads together. We have many clues and a few suspects. Remember, we need means, motive and opportunity. I created this matrix to illustrate our web of intrigue. To be thorough, we will review from the beginning to ensure no stone is left unturned."

"Does she always do this?" Private Eyes asked quietly to Daring Detective.

"Yes." Daring muffled her laugh with her hand over her face.

"Let's review the suspects," I presented.

"Binny Buttercup was a scorned lover who threatened revenge on Willow in public. He was known to bring her drinks. He could have easily poisoned her.

"Like I said, hell hath no fury like a man scorned?" Mayhem laughed.

"I think you said a woman before," Private Eyes corrected.

"Well, we interviewed Binny and some of his harem of women and we found none of the speculation to be probable. He's just a sweet guy," Daring explained.

"Even a sweet guy can be pushed into a crime of passion," Sir Red Herring said.

"Yes, but..." Daring started to say when she was interrupted by Inspector Instinct.

"People heard him threaten her."

"He explained that!" Private eyes exclaimed.

"Yes, he made it clear that he was concerned about her welfare with the young gigolo. He thought he would fleece her for all her money—her inheritance. No one thinks he could have done it," Daring said in a calm voice, motioning to Private Eyes to keep her cool.

"If he poisoned her or even kidnapped her, what did he do with her?" Smoking Gun added coolly.

"Right. We were in his home and saw nothing," Private Eyes affirmed with a defiant nod.

"Very well. We'll keep him in mind. Let's discuss the next suspect, Petunia Periwinkle," I directed.

"Petunia didn't do it!" Minx shouted.

"Miss Minx, we must follow every possible trail until it comes to a natural conclusion," I said.

"Or a dead end," Mayhem laughed.

"Mr. Mayhem. You are on shaky ground here. If you do not cease with these pointless puns, I will eradicate you from this elite group," I ordered. "Now, Miss Minx, what did we find out about Ms. Periwinkle?"

"I know Petunia and I interviewed her personally. She did not like Willow, that is true, and she did argue with her, but she didn't kill her," Minx said with absolute confidence.

"Well, how do you know she didn't kill her?" Mayhem asked.

"She's eighty years old and much smaller than Willow. How exactly did she lift her into an incinerator? And I think we all know that you can fit a person in a trash chute," Minx said with some sarcasm.

"Good point. I think the physicality of the deed makes the means implausible, if not impossible. Petunia is off the list," I directed.

"What about Willow's shoe found near the incinerator?" Herring asked.

"It could have gone down the garbage chute and just missed the bin. In my building, that happens all the time when the incinerator fills up. They only light it twice a week," Private Eyes said.

"Excellent deduction. Now to Iris Impatiens. She had means, motive and opportunity. What did you find, Magnolia?" I asked.

"Well, Iris definitely had the means. We found broken railing pieces at the old bridge and have two reliable sources who saw them together walking to the bridge. Plus, we found a phone with a red floral case and a red golf visor on the creek bank," Magnolia said.

"How do we know it's Willow's phone?" Cluemaster asked.

"My photographic memory earned me the title of reigning southwest Florida jigsaw champ three years in a row. I saw Willow with that red floral phone case many times in the arts and crafts room. It's unusual and definitely Willow's," Delta nodded with certainty.

"But we're still unclear about the motive. All we have is a fight over a ruined pot," Magnolia added.

"A ruined pot? Like pottery? That's a red herring if I ever heard one," Herring chuckled.

"Well now, bless your heart, Red," Magnolia smiled wryly.

"Right, the motive is improbable. And everyone we interviewed about Iris said she's not prone to violence and had no trouble with anyone else, except Willow," Delta added.

"Her husband said that Iris called Willow a bitch," Smoking Gun said with a cynical look. "Can we talk about the real case now?"

"I looked into the idea of a missing senior ring, but that was a bust," Newshound asked.

"Conspiracy theories? While we've been doing real detective work, you want to discuss aliens who abduct seniors?" Sparks said.

"Why not? Alien abduction is real!" Delta shouted in response.

"Not aliens—senior trafficking, I have accounts of several incidents in the area. I still think if we threw a broad net, we could find something," Newshound insisted.

"What are they trafficking them for? Sex? Workhouses? Do you hear how ridiculous you sound?" Cluemaster said and threw up his hands.

"Ladies and gentlemen! Let us have some order here. We substantiated all the reports of missing persons and only Willow Wisteria remains absent, so I believe we can lay the senior trafficking theory to rest in this case. But I would like to hear more about those accounts for future reference, Mr. Newshound," I said. "Newshound is to be congratulated for saving that diabetic man's life. See, people? Sleuthing saves lives."

"Thank you. I also discovered her mailbox was empty, so someone was picking up her mail," Newshound added, somewhat defeated.

"If she's dead, it would be hard for her to pick up her mail," Mayhem chided.

"Finally," Inspector Instinct said, frustrated. "I think we can all concede that many people hated her, but we are wasting time with this fruitless witch hunt. The real criminal is Willow. We are dealing with dubious outside forces here."

"Succinctly stated, Inspector. Please illuminate us on your findings," I agreed.

"We found out Willow is flush with cash. We found one hundred thousand dollars in her condo alone and she pays cash for everything. We also believe she was selling liquid CBD and marijuana from her home. We believe the two men, the gigolos, were her accomplices," Instinct said.

"Everything traces back to a company in New York called the Happy Endings Massage Company, which is connected to a New York crime family," Smoking Gun explained.

"Happy Endings Massage Company is a great front to cover the contraband in the boxes. No one is going to open those boxes for fear of what they would find," Mayhem said, and a few others laughed along with him.

"Even so, she wouldn't leave all those boxes in front of her door on purpose with drugs in them. Something must have happened to her," Minx added.

"Agreed. This is definitely the best option to pursue. I must admit I'm relieved that the perpetrator is not living among us. Smoking Gun, what did you find out about the company?" I asked.

"That's an interesting story. Crime has penetrated our little community." Smoking Gun sat back in his chair.

"The potential hit-and-run car is registered to the Happy Endings Massage Company in New York, Willow's supplier and also a connection to an unpleasant New York family who supposedly smuggles all kinds of goods. I sent a picture of our restaurant neighbor to some friends and they identified him as an old-school mid-level player in the family. If his wife recognized Willow, bada bing, there's a connection," Smoking Gun concluded.

"Excellent deductive diligence! It appears all roads lead to Willow as a drug dealer. The cash, the product peddling, the accomplices, and the mob connection. That leaves our suspects as the gigolos or the mafia. But we still don't know if she's dead and which ones did the deed," I concluded.

"We didn't find any traces of poison, so I believe we can eliminate that," Cluist said.

"These kinds of guys don't poison people. They use muscle," Smoking Gun chuckled.

"Indeed. Was anyone able to track down these gigolos?" I asked.

"No, I've been looking at camera footage and talking to the gate security. There's no sign of that young man or the Porsche guy since Willow disappeared," Sparks said.

"They just vanished into thin air," Mayhem quipped.

"What about the mob? Are there any more clues there?" Daring asked.

"I assure you, the mob has been covering their tracks for years. You'll never nail them," Smoking Gun said.

"Then it seems like we've hit a dead end, so to speak," Daring said, and everyone looked at each other with blank stares.

"Well, let's not give up yet. We've done some wonderful work here, but the solution still eludes us. Put on your thinking caps. There must be a way to find the perpetrator. Let's reconvene tomorrow afternoon at three o'clock precisely to discuss," I directed.

"I can't meet at three, Madame. I have an exercise class," Daring said.

"Yes, and I have tap class," Magnolia added.

"Very well, we will meet at one o'clock precisely," I said.

"I have a tennis game," Minx and Quister said at the same time.

"And Herring and I are in a ping pong tournament until five p.m.," Mayhem said.

"Well, something has to give here, people. How can I run a secret sleuths society if everyone just wants to have fun?" I said, frustrated. "Then make it five o'clock. Hearing no objection, we will reconvene tomorrow at five p.m. Dismissed."

Chapter 14

The Visitor:

Madame Sleuth

Before our meeting, I received a call from our community manager. He forwarded a message from the FBI. They wanted to meet me here and discuss our investigation. I'm not sure how they found out, but apparently our inquiries raised some red flags. I hope everyone was careful, but in the end, my fingerprints were not on anything.

"Madame Sleuth? I'm Agent Athos of the FBI. I heard you're working on the disappearance of Willow Wisteria."

"Well, we were just making some small inquiries. Many people in the community were upset by the idea of one of our residents being abducted or even killed. We were just doing our part to keep the peace," I said innocently and understated our involvement because I didn't want our group to be on the FBI's radar. It would shut us down completely.

"Well, I will need you to stand down and provide me with any information you have. This is a federal matter now," he ordered.

"As a matter of fact, I have everything here, as we are meeting shortly. But I have to admit, curiosity has killed the cat in this case. Isn't there anything you can tell us…or even just me? I give you my solemn personal pledge that I will not divulge any detail," I asked.

"We at the FBI are not in the habit of giving out information to civilians," he said coolly.

I handed him a thumb drive Sparks gave me with the master camera files, the paper files of all the social media posts that I indexed and color-coded and a summary of the notes we took on all of our deductions and interviews. And, of course, my web of clues.

I didn't want to give it all up, but the FBI has spies everywhere. We didn't want to make them an enemy and it could be beneficial in the future to have a friend in the FBI.

"Here are all the files, Agent Athos. Are you sure you can't disclose anything?" I fervently asked again.

"You have accumulated a lot of interesting information here." He looked concerned as he scanned the files. "Well, I'm not supposed to do this, but you've been so helpful. Let's just say I forgot this folder here and maybe you saw it, read it and destroyed it. For your eyes only." Agent Athos said and left the room.

I hated to see our first real case end like this. I spent days and days of time and effort into the entire mystery. I was heartbroken to think it would go unanswered and unresolved. But, as long as I know what happened, it was really solved.

I looked around and grabbed the folder. I couldn't wait to open it. The manila file folder was marked "Top Secret. Code name: Willow Wisteria." Inside there was a transcript which said it was recorded phone conversation on a secure line…

Willow: I just don't understand why I have to be inconvenienced again. Is this my life now, like a nomad? A drifter?

Athos: Well, you could be a little nicer to everyone and make friends, not enemies.

Willow: I have no idea what you're talking about. I am a delight. I have tons of friends.

Athos: Really? We track the social media in the area and everyone's talking about you. And this sleuths society put together a list of who did you in and how…and it's a long list.

Willow: People are just jealous.

Athos: Well, at least keep a low profile this time.

Willow: I always do.

Athos: Are you kidding? You should read some of this.

Willow: I never indulge in gossip.

Athos: You were made, and they tried to take you out. Do you think it was an accident?

Willow: Well, at least go back and get my things. You let me take so little and it was so rushed; I left my golf cart at the club and one of my favorite shoes fell out of my bag.

Athos: We took care of the golf cart. Red and flowers? That's not exactly keeping a low profile.

Willow: It's my color. I'm an autumn. And what about my packages?

Athos: Yeah, and about that. Knock off that therapy stuff. You attract too much attention.

Willow: Well, I have to have something to do. And besides, senior sex therapy is a perfectly legitimate profession. I help a lot of people and save marriages.

Athos: Couldn't you just sell Avon or something? With all those packages, someone would think you're still in the smuggling business.

Willow: Of course not. That's what got me into this situation. My life has never my own since I testified against the boss. I need my tools. Senior sex therapy is a sticky business.

Athos: Just be nice this time, okay?

Oooo! This is juicy. How exciting! She was a sex therapist…and she was in witness protection.

This explained a lot - the shoe, the golf cart, the packages, the mob, the hit-and-run and all the men coming in and out of her condo.

We were on the right track on some things, and a few of us really went off the rails on others. I needed to fix that for the next case. We just didn't have all the pieces to the puzzle.

The case was solved now. I felt a little bad keeping it from the others. They worked very hard on the case…but then again, so did I and he did say for my eyes only. What kind of presiding investigator would I be if I couldn't keep a secret? Especially a secret as delightfully decadent as this one.

Chapter 15

The Solution:

Madame Sleuth

"Ladies and gentlemen, we came here to discuss the case, but some new video footage just came into our possession from a home security CCTV camera of a home on the golf course. It's hard to see, but that is Willow Wisteria on the golf course at night," I announced.

Alien 1: This is the place to find the seniors.

Alien 2: Look, there's one.

Alien 1: Good, grab her. Now we can force her to buy us cheap movie tickets and hotel rooms with her AARP discounts.

Alien 2: Hurry, before someone issues one of those Silver Alerts.

Alien 1: I told you we should have brought the black spaceship instead of the silver one.

"SEE! I knew it!! Alien abduction is a real thing. Call the police. Call NASA. Call the FBI." Delta jumped up out of her chair and yelled.

"Delta Snoops, get a hold of yourself! I mean the very idea," I said, surprised at her reaction.

"No, it didn't happen like that. But wouldn't that have been funny? My grandson made up this video on his little computer. I thought a little levity would be welcome," I said.

"But I have some exciting and disturbing news. The good news is our inquiries on this case attracted some unexpected attention. Management was contacted by the FBI and I received a visit today from Agent Athos. The bad news is the FBI ordered us off the case and took all our information, notes and videos. We are under strict directions not to discuss the case or any of its information again," I explained.

"They took everything? How can they do that?" Sir Red Herring asked.

"They can definitely do that," Captain Cluemaster added.

"If the FBI is involved, it's got to be big," Inspector Instinct said.

"We did all this work for nothing?" Mayhem objected.

"I guess so, but why did they shut the case on us? What happened to Willow?" Daring Detective asked.

"Yes, we need to know what happened," Delta demanded.

"I know this is disappointing, but know this, I assembled a crack team, and no professional detective agency would have done a better job. The FBI agent was very impressed and a little distressed at all the information we uncovered. But the fact is, we are civilians and this is now a government matter," I declared.

"We'll never find out what happened. The feds are very tight-lipped. Guess this case is a bust," Smoking Gun said and left the room.

"That stinks, but I have to admit, this was really fun," Private Eyes said.

"Exactly, we have all stretched our investigative muscles and know we have the capacity for crime-solving. There will be more official and unofficial opportunities to crack capers and decode, decipher and deduce detective work in the future. We have only just begun. The best is yet to come. Everyone is dismissed with my thanks," I said and the group left grumbling.

I was alone in the empty room. Again, I felt a smidgeon of guilt that I knew the real truth, but I was sworn to secrecy. I couldn't help that.

The Case of the Vanishing Vixen was now a closed book in what will certainly be the long annals of the history of the Secret Senior Sleuths Society.

Now, as presiding investigator, it was my duty to look forward to the next case.

I needed to check the cameras again to see what secrets were out there right now. Did they really think I would get rid of those cameras? Not a chance—they are the lifeblood of my work. Senior communities are full of misdeeds and mystery; you just need to know where to look.

"Madame, the police are at Pheasant villas." Queens Quister came bursting into the room. "The neighbors said someone found a dead body and a barking dog left on the lanai alone. I wonder if it's a murder? Hurry!"

I grabbed my purse and headed out the door. We had an actual body this time—how exciting. We could do so much more investigative work with a real corpse.

We'll have to see what we can do about the police, though. That will make it more difficult.

Back to work…our next case. I know; I'll call it "The Peril at Peacock Perch."

Chapter 16

The Ruse:

Willow Wisteria

Athos said he pulled it off. The old windbag fell for it. I couldn't believe she really thought he was from the FBI. Ha! She gave him everything. Those young Greek gods could get anything from women.

Madame Sleuth and her feeble band of amateur dicks were no match for a pro. They were a nuisance, but now they wouldn't blow the lid off my operation.

Sometimes I wish I were in witness protection. It would be easier if the Feds had to pay for everything and set me up again when the heat is on. But then I would have to squeal on someone. No chance of that. This time, it was too close. In my mind, there was a difference between squealing and stealing, but my old bosses didn't seem to think so.

They were still sore just because I took a little on the side. I worked hard. I deserved a few hundred thousand extra just for organizing those crazy asinine Christmas parties every year. The boss's wife came up with some real doozie theme ideas, like "Christmas in the Tropics" where we had a luau with Polynesian music and everyone had to dress like they were extras in *South Pacific*.

But the worst was "A Country Christmas." Imagine a bunch of city slickers dressed like hayseeds. That alone should've earned me the cool mil in seed money I appropriated to grow my magic recipes and proliferate them to the poor masses.

Do you believe they put a hit out on me just for that? That gang spends more than that on jewelry.

That stupid numb nut and his dopey wife pegged me and tried to take me out.

Good thing my New York contacts found out about it first. Someone drove all the way down here and pretended to abduct me just to throw them off the scent. Even with my sneakers on, I had to run and jump to make it look realistic.

I escaped only by the hair of my chinny-chin-chin. Now I needed to set up my operation with a new set of suckers. Senior communities were the perfect place to hock my "herbal" remedies, but every new place I had to start all over again with a new persona. Plus, I had to cultivate new customers.

Word of mouth was my only option. It's not like I could advertise. It was a good thing the boys weren't made, so we had some regulars on the outside they could still sell to until I get established in another retirement joint.

Where are those two guys? They were supposed to meet me here already.

"Boss, here's your new credit cards and driver's license. Your name this time is Ginger Gardenia," Athos said.

"I just love these flower and tree names. I think I'll dye my hair red this time to fit the name," I laughed.

"And I cleaned out the condo and had our friends sell it and both cars. The new cars arrive tomorrow. I guess I'll drive a red corvette now instead of a Porsche," Georgio said.

"Good, I underestimated that senior sleuths society at Peacock Perch. They nearly figured it all out. I won't do that again. We need to keep track of social media better this time to keep tabs on people," I said and dismissed the boys.

Social media could be a great tool, but it nearly sank me last time. I had to sneak a few fake posts in just to throw them off the scent. Ha! They actually fell for that "eaten by an alligator" bit. But at least that made sense. Aliens, though? Ha! What saps…pure genius on my part.

I played all those chumps like a fiddle. I even got that English pippy neighbor of mine to think I was being snatched. I knew she could overhear everything I said on my balcony. I figured she was always snooping on me. What else did she have to do? Drink tea?

Setting up a new shop was always such a pain. I had to reestablish everything, get involved with the people, playing their incessant card games and joining their insipid groups. The only thing I really liked was the weekly dances, but I hoped this group didn't have a line dancing club. I hated line dancers!

But I wanted to gain their confidence so I could sell to them. I sold three times as much here as the boys did on the outside. Maybe I should change the name of my company, but since I started the secret cover as a sex therapist, my sales tripled.

I found that both men and women are really interested in my sex therapy secrets. I talked to them at events and games and then I sold them my "special" lotions and oils. Chit chat was a very effective tool for sales. One person told another and business boomed. People were much happier when they loosen up. Plus, it helped everything that ails them, inside and outside the boudoir.

I needed to make sure my New York contacts have my new address. The Happy Endings Massage Company rides again. Now, I just had to find out when bingo was.

Secret Senior Sleuths
Society Series

What's Next?

Now that *The Case of the Vanishing Vixen* is solved, the society got their first taste of a real case and they are ready for more. Luckily, as Madame Sleuth says, senior communities are full of misdeeds and mystery and this group knows where to find their next whodunit.

You met our kooky band of wannabe sleuths. They'll be back in the second book in the series, *Peril in Peacock Perch*.

In the second book, the society tackles the suspicious death of a resident leading the group to suspect foul play. While the police rule the death as natural causes, scuttlebutt in the community and an interesting series of clues take the society down the path to investigate and find out for themselves. Was the resident murdered?

There are several unresolved or mentioned Easter egg clues in this book that preview what's coming up. Can you guess what they are?

Subscribe to my newsletter at www.suzanneruddhamilton.com for exclusive news and sneak peeks on this and more books coming soon. Newsletter subscribers will also get a free link to live clips of the play *Puzzle at Peacock Perch*, which inspired the book, where you can see the secret camera footage and endings play out on film.

About the Author

Thank you for reading this book. I am a mystery junkie too, but I try to connect the dots with some humor and heart. Nothing is ever what it seems. I encourage everyone to make their own path in life, no matter what age. I did, but it took a long time.

I spent my first career trying to find my bliss in journalism, public relations, real estate, and marketing. Now I'm enjoying my second career—writing. I write in many genres for all ages, but I always try to tell stories of everyday life experiences in a fun-filled read. Originally from Chicago, my husband, dog and I, along with my computer, are happy transplants in the warm and gentle breezes of Southwest Florida.

Please let me know what you think with a review on Amazon.com   https://www.amazon.com/review/create-review?&asin=B09JDGMYGC or Goodreads.com or a note on any of the social media channels below. I value the opinions of my readers and will always strive to entertain and give you a good feeling after the last page is read. Check out my available works on the next page.

Feel free to reach out to me on my social media channels and sign up for my newsletter to get weekly short stories, bonus materials, name and book cover reveals and contests, giveaways, and exclusive sneak peeks and updates on new releases. I love to hear from my readers. You can sign up and find out what I'm working on and get some behind the pages information at www.suzanneruddhamilton.com. You can also follow me on social media at:

 @suzanneruddhamilton

 @suzanneruddhamilton

 @suzruddhamilton

 Suzanne Rudd Hamilton, Author

 @suzanneruddhamilton

 @suzanneruddhamilton

My Other Works

Welcome to my world. I write cozy mysteries, women's fiction, romances, books for middle grades and young adults and children's illustrated books under a couple of derivatives of my name. My books are clean and friendly for any audience. If you want to read more from me, here are my works. All novels are available in paperback and eBook on Amazon.com and Kindle and soon to be available as audiobooks through Amazon.com/Audible:

Cozy/Detective Mystery: Suzanne Rudd Hamilton

Beck's Rules Mysteries Series:

– *Beck's Rules*

– When Walls Talk: Beck's Rules 2 (2022 release)

Secret Senior Sleuths Society Series:

– Puzzle at Peacock Perch

Historical Romance: Suzanne Rudd Hamilton

Current Series:
A *Timeless* American Historical Romance
– *The Sailor and the Songbird*

Women's Fiction: Suzanne Rudd Hamilton
New Series: The *Little Shoppes* Books
- Cupcakes, Etc. (2021 release)

Middle-Grade/Young Adult: Suzanne Rudd
Current Series: Growing Up Girls
– *Diary of a 6th Grade "C" Cup*
– *The One and Only Skizitz*

Children's Picture Books: Suzanne Hamilton

– *How an Angel Gets Its Wings*

I also write plays for the performing arts: *Hollywood Whodunnit*; *Death, Debauchery and Dinner*; *Dames are Dangerous*; and *Puzzle at Peacock Perch* – as well as a new musical, *Welcome Home*.

With Love and Appreciation

This book is dedicated to my family and friends who helped me break down obstacles, jump over hurdles, and leap ahead—and who picked me up each time I got knocked down.

Thanks to my "Pens" and other writer friends and colleagues for your encouragement and direction. And to my editor Andie and cover artist Elizabeth, who are my safety nets.

And to my drama group, thanks for the idea and support in the creation of this series and your continued perseverance to bring my creations to life on stage.

Printed in Great Britain
by Amazon

72447511R00108